ABOUT THIS BOOK

Celeste is used to getting her way—it comes naturally. Now that she's coming of age, she's about to learn why things turn out in her favor so often, and find out some hidden truths about her own identity. She'd better learn fast how to keep her nature under control, before it gets her kicked out of town—or worse.

Jonathan has been on the run for as long as he can remember. Everything he's been taught was in service of keeping his family's secret safe. And this isn't just any family secret—if it gets out, it could mean the destruction of his people. He and his mom hope Havenwood Falls will be a safe haven for them and the secret they protect. But they may have run right into the hands of their enemies.

When Celeste sets her sights on Jonathan, she may be in for her biggest challenge yet. He can't afford a distraction like dating. But every time their paths cross, they're drawn closer together. Let the battle of wills begin.

HAVENWOOD FALLS HIGH BOOKS

Paper Bird by Amy Richie

Predestined by Valia Lind

Rediscovered by Morgan Wylie

Ashes of Fate by Apryl Baker

Stay up to date at www.HavenwoodFalls.com

WILLFUL

A HAVENWOOD FALLS HIGH NOVELLA

LIZ FERRY

For my willful child

PROLOGUE

JONATHAN

*I*t was a bright, sunny day when it happened. If it had been rainy, we would have stayed home, and they would have caught us. But it was cool and crisp, and Mom wanted to take a stroll down to the open-air market to pick up some fresh vegetables. She usually went with Mrs. Viegas, our neighbor, a nice old lady who'd lived in the small mountain town for her whole life, but today she asked me to walk with her, and I did, because I was bored.

We walked along the cobblestone streets, Mom drilling me on history facts, dodging kids playing and women sweeping their stoops. At the market, surrounded by the earthy smells of farm-fresh produce, we picked up tomatoes and cucumbers, onions and potatoes, celery and cabbage. At every booth, Mom stopped to chat with the farmers, asking about their children, their harvest, and their health.

On our way back from the market with a bag full of vegetables, we ran into Mrs. Viegas hurrying down the road. She stopped us with waving arms, but lowered voice. She spoke into my mother's ear for a minute, and I watched my mom's expression turn to panic, matching the old lady's, as her hand came up to clutch the gold pendant she

1

wore. My mother started nodding rapidly, then shoved the bag of vegetables into our neighbor's arms and grabbed my hand.

"*Obrigada, obrigada,*" my mother thanked Mrs. Viegas, then turned and ran, dragging me along with her.

I was surprised at the speed with which we were able to leave town. Apparently, Mom had set up contingency plans for getting us out if—when—we needed to run. We ran to Mr. Mata's garage, where my mother pulled him out from under a car and told him she needed her keys. He ran to the office and handed over a set of keys, then pointed to the back door of the shop. Within minutes, we were out of town and speeding down the road to Lisbon.

About half an hour after we left, I looked out the back window to see a thin plume of black smoke rising into the sky above the town that had been our home for the last three years. I hoped Mrs. Viegas was okay.

CHAPTER 1

CELESTE

"Celeste! Finally," Margaret said as she opened the door. Her mass of black curls was held back with a thin pink headband, which matched her chiffon dress.

"That's what you're wearing?" I bypassed polite greetings and got straight to the point. "No, no, no. Come on, we still have time," I continued, marching through the front door and up the stairs to Margaret's room, with my friend trailing along behind me.

"What's wrong with it?" asked Margaret. I could tell she was already resigned to the fact that her pale pink party dress from Dress Perfect would be spending the night back on its hanger.

"Well, first, you wore it to Christine's birthday party six months ago. And second, it's . . ." I trailed off, looking the dress up and down, trying to find a way to tell her it would send her crush entirely the wrong message. Catching Margaret's disappointed expression, I softened my tone. "It's just not flirty enough. Tonight's not just the Sweetheart Dance, it's your first date with Xavier. You've got to show off those curves! Remind him how lucky he is that he landed a date with you."

"Oh . . . yeah, I guess you're right," Margaret conceded, looking to her closet worriedly and adjusting her glasses. "But what will I—"

"Where's that little black dress we got at Callie's?" I interrupted, impatiently flipping through the hangers in the closet.

"Behind the door, but—"

"But what?" I asked, turning to pull the dress, still wrapped in its plastic cover, off the back of the closet door.

"It's so . . . short," Margaret admitted, her eyes glued to the hemline.

I looked at my friend and closed the mirrored closet door in front of her. "Margie," I leveled in my best no-nonsense voice. "Look at those legs. Hike up that long-ass skirt you're wearing and look."

Margaret obliged, shrugging.

"You've got gorgeous gams, girl! You can't not show those things off."

"Gams?" Margaret laughed. "Who says that?"

I giggled. "I couldn't resist. Look at this fantastic flapper dress! I'd be dying to wear this! It's perfect for tonight."

Margaret held up the vintage twenties gown, complete with black fringe and crystal beading. It really was beautiful, and Callie had sworn it was authentic.

"Okay," Margaret caved. "Find me some shoes."

Suppressing a squeal of glee, I dove back into the closet in search of footwear while Margaret changed, and came up with a pair of strappy black heels that were hidden under a mountain of flats. I helped pin her curls into a stylish twist on top of her head, watching her transform from awkward teen to sophisticated young woman before my eyes.

"Perfect!" I exclaimed when Margaret stepped into the shoes and twirled, the fringe floating around her. "Xavier's going to melt, you're so hot."

"Speaking of hot," Margaret said, grabbing her extra-long coat, "I'll need this so I don't turn to ice—and to make it past my dad."

We laughed our way back down the stairs arm in arm, Margaret's shoulders loosening with every step, then freezing when the doorbell rang.

"It's him," Margaret said.

We made it through the obligatory stern looks from Margaret's dad and piled into Xavier's car. Even though it wasn't far to the Annex (nothing was really *far* in our little town), it was too icy to walk more than a block or two in heels.

By the time we got to the Annex, my mood had turned from giddy to glum. I walked into the building wondering why I was even there. With no sweetheart to bring to the Sweetheart Dance, why bother? As I watched Xavier's eyes nearly bug out of his head when Margaret slipped out of her coat, though, I remembered, and I couldn't keep a smile from my lips. My friend had been pining after the object of her desire for months, and I was happy to finally see them on the right track.

Handing my own coat over at the coat check table, I smoothed my hands over my silver sheath dress and looked around. Now that the important part was over with, I'd have to make the best of the evening.

The space inside the Annex had been rearranged to accommodate the event, and I had to admit the decorating committee had done a great job. The stage at the far end was set up for one of the better local bands, the Mountain Monsters, but just now the DJ, on a separate dais to the right, was playing upbeat music and taking requests for slow dances later on.

I turned to my left and headed for the refreshments table. As I turned back with a plastic cup of pink punch, someone walking in the door caught my eye. Someone new.

I watched as he stopped short of the dance floor and appeared to scan the crowd for a familiar face. His shaggy blond hair shone in the multicolored lights, and long lashes framed pale blue eyes. He was in a sleek black leather jacket and dark jeans. As I watched, he ran his fingers through that hair, sending shivers down my spine.

5

"Are you going to stand there like a statue all night, Celeste, or come show us your moves?" A voice beside me shook me out of my guy-ogling reverie.

"Emma, you're here!" I said a little too loudly. "Just hydrating before dancing," I covered, raising my cup to my lips and hoping she hadn't seen my eyes glued to the hottie.

"Well, finish that and come on! We need you in our girl circle of power," Emma said, her long light brown hair pulled into a sleek braid down her back, with curled tendrils framing her heart-shaped face.

Nodding, I drained my cup and turned to put it on the table behind her, surreptitiously taking another peek toward the entrance. A steady stream of people now flowed in through the door, but the new guy was nowhere to be seen.

I let my friends drag me out to the dance floor and tried to put the guy out of my mind. I hadn't found one yet who had held my interest past the first conversation. No doubt this one would be the same. I reminded myself to live in the moment and enjoy the night out, and to stop searching the crowd for a leather jacket.

"Dad, I'm home," I called as I walked in the door. I lived with my father in a modest two-bedroom house on Third Street, a short walk from both the high school and Miller's Plaza, where my dad's office was. He was a business accountant, keeping the books and doing taxes for several of the small businesses around town.

"You're home early," Dad replied, coming out of his study, where he spent most of his evenings during tax season. "How was the dance?"

"Oh, fine, just the same kids I see at school every day all dressed up," I said, hanging my coat by the door. Looking up to see my father's eyebrows pinched together, I quickly readjusted my own expression into a believable smile. "Fun. It was fun."

His face relaxed into a mirror of my own, and he gave a quick nod.

"Good, well, there's lasagna in the fridge if you're hungry. I've got some more forms to finish up," he said, heading back toward his desk.

I went to my own room, getting ready for bed while I pondered a set of blue eyes framed by long lashes.

∾

EVEN THOUGH I absolutely intended to sleep in on Friday, since we had a four-day weekend for Presidents' Day, I was up as usual at six in the morning. Unable to fall back to sleep, I got ready for my day. Emma, Gianna, and I had plans to go skiing later, but I had a few hours to kill, so I left a note for my dad, whom I could hear in the shower, and walked toward the town square. The sun was out, and the mountain air was fresh and mild. It would be a great day to hit the slopes.

I walked into Broastful Brew and ordered a coffee and a muffin, then settled in at my favorite corner table. It was a busy weekday morning, but early enough that most of the high school kids were probably still in bed. The town square was decorated with an explosion of heart decorations in pink and red. A beautiful woman with long black hair strode through the park in heels, still dressed in her slinky gown from the night before. I liked the peaceful, quiet vibe in the coffeehouse. I occasionally went to the other coffee shop in the square, Coffee Haven, if I happened to be shopping nearby, but I could have sworn I caught Willow giving me strange sideways looks whenever I went in there. It gave me the creeps. Mabel, the owner of Broastful Brew, always had a smile and a kind word for everyone.

As I gazed out at the square, I tuned out the conversations around me, until Irene Beckett's voice sounded from the table just behind me. She was a little old lady who used to teach at the high school decades ago and still thought she had the right to tell everyone how to live.

"Is that Tasha Young doing the walk of shame this morning?"

I glanced over to see her breakfast companion, Sybil Carson, who was always an eager audience for Mrs. Beckett's gossip. Usually they hung out at Coffee Haven, but I guessed they were here gathering information on someone or another.

"It looks more like a walk of pride to me," Sybil replied with a smile.

"Well, it's too bad she was never my student," Irene said, "or I'd have talked some decency into her. Look at that dress! It's fit for a—"

"Can I get you ladies anything else?" Mabel broke into their conversation just as Mrs. Beckett was about to lose her composure. I hid a giggle behind another bite of my muffin.

"No, thank you, dear," Mrs. Beckett said with an edge in her voice. "Have you seen the new woman in town yet? She's got a teenage son— it's just the two of them—and they just arrived this week."

"No," Mabel sighed, "they haven't been in here. I heard they're staying with Mrs. Walsh, so they probably go over to Coffee Haven for their caffeine."

"Well, don't you worry about that," Mrs. Beckett said. "One bite of those cookies, and they'll be hooked!"

"Why, thank you, Irene. Now I'd better get back to the counter. Let me know if you need anything!"

I focused back on my coffee. A new family in town, just this week. Could it be the guy I had spotted at the dance last night? I had kept an eye out for him the rest of the evening, but hadn't seen him again. I was beginning to think he was just an illusion.

Shrugging off the thought, I cleared my dishes to the counter and waved goodbye to Mabel. If he was at the dance, he'd be at school, and I'd find out soon enough who he was. But I had more important things to worry about. Like getting my ski on.

CHAPTER 2

CELESTE

*I*t seemed like half the high school was out on the slopes already as I rode the ski lift up Mount Mae with Emma and Gianna.

"So are you ready for Hell or High Water, Celeste?" Gianna asked, referring to the double black diamond trail on the slope we were ascending.

"I want to warm up on a blue square first, then we'll see," I said. "It's been too long since I was out here. Not like you two ski bunnies. How about starting on Renae's Way?"

My friends looked at each other and nodded. "Sure," they said in unison. I loved how easygoing they were.

"How late did you guys stay at the dance last night?" I asked, watching Emma stifle a yawn.

"Oh, they shut it down at eleven. But we went to Gianna's afterward and watched *Thor*." She got a dreamy look in her eye. "I wish I knew some movie stars."

This prompted a giggle from Gianna. "Look around, Emma. There are plenty of beautiful people in town. Some of them are even our own age!"

She pointed to the group of skiers waiting for a turn on the slope as we reached the end of the lift. I looked over and spotted Laurel Alverson chatting up Brice Blackstone, and Samuel Milton sneaking glances at Aurelia Petran.

"Yeah, but they're all so . . . ordinary," Emma whined. At this, Gianna burst out laughing, and didn't stop until we reached the top of the trail. She did tend to have an odd sense of humor at times.

I took the first run, and met my girls at the bottom to board the ski lift again, after which we proceeded to ski the black diamonds for the rest of the afternoon. We had all grown up in Havenwood Falls, where skiing was one of the few available pastimes in the winter, so we had all become rather good at it, if not quite experts.

It being Friday, there weren't many adults on the slopes, but there were a few couples who had taken a long weekend and were being all lovey-dovey in the crisp mountain air. Mesmerized, we all watched Rusty Higgins zig and zag as he descended the mountain. Sherry winked at us when he turned out of sight and smacked her lips as she prepared to follow him down.

After the sun was long past its peak, we were lined up at the top of the Hell or High Water trail for what would be one of the last runs of the day. Emma was telling us about her plans for spring break—she was going to Maui with her family—and the woman in front of us kept looking back.

"Do you girls think you're ready for this trail?" she finally asked.

Gianna, Emma, and I looked at each other, stunned at this woman's gall, and burst out laughing.

"Yeah, I think so," I managed to get out after the hilarity died down a bit, "since this is our fourth run up here today."

"Well, maybe you should spend more time focusing and less time chattering," she snipped. "This course requires focus, and you'd do well to respect it."

I gaped. Who did this woman think she was? I put on my sweetest smile. "We are so glad that tourists like you are here to educate us on our slopes. Oh, look, it's your turn. Best focus on your skiing, now. We wouldn't want you to have an accident."

She harrumphed—really!—and turned around to descend the slope. We watched her in stony silence as she collected herself and then took off down the side of the mountain. I narrowed my eyes, cursing her in my head, watching for some flaw in her technique I could taunt her about when we ran into her at the bottom. Were her legs too far apart? All of a sudden, her left foot shot out, the ski catching a stray patch of ice and sending her tumbling toward the tree line.

Everyone gasped as she crashed into a tree. Judging by the force with which she hit, she definitely broke an arm, maybe a rib or two as well.

An employee from the ski resort arrived and called for paramedics. We watched sadly as he then closed off the run for the day.

"Sorry, folks," he said. "Head down that way for the next run." He pointed across the mountain to the next trail, and we all tromped off toward it.

I shot a glance back at the woman crumpled against the tree and found her glaring at me. As if *I* was responsible for her mishap. Shaking my head, I continued on after my friends. *Some people will blame anyone but themselves.*

"Well, I'm done," Gianna said when we reached the end of the next run. "I've got a family dinner to go to tonight, and I'll catch hell if I'm late."

"Are we still on for tomorrow night?" Emma asked, taking off her hat and combing fingers through her straight hair. We had made plans to meet at Margaret's house for a movie marathon and sleepover.

"Yes, definitely," Gianna said. "I'll bring the popcorn."

Emma grinned at me as we made our way back to the parking lot. She loved getting the girls together at every opportunity, and this weekend was like a dream for her.

I arrived home to a dark house. Even though it was almost six, my dad was still at his office. He would be working for another hour or two, so I went in and turned on all the lights, to make me feel less alone. The truth was, though, I needed some time to myself. Spending all day with my friends was fun but draining. Funny as it may sound, I felt as though I was constantly monitoring their moods and making sure they had a good time. It was like I'd been directing traffic for hours. I shook my head to clear the strange feeling and refocus, then warmed up some leftover lasagna and settled in on the sofa to watch TV.

I woke with a start when my dad arrived home, slamming the door behind him and muttering something about motorcycles and not respecting traffic laws.

"Hi, Dad."

"Hmm." It was more a grunt than a response. I tried again.

"Everything okay at work today?"

"One month until business taxes are due, and I still don't have receipts from half my clients. Half!" he began to rant. "You know they'll all magically come up with them a week before the deadline, and I'll be stuck working around the clock to get everything done on time."

"Life of an accountant?"

He scoffed. "Yeah, well, it gets older every year. Why can't people be more organized? I'm not a machine!"

"I know, Daddy. People are the absolute worst."

His face softened as he looked at me. "Ah well, without them, where would I be, eh?" He nodded at my empty plate, still on the living room coffee table. "Sorry I didn't make it home in time for dinner, Celeste."

"Oh, it's no biggie. I was famished after spending all day up on Mount Mae."

"Ah, I forgot you were heading up there today. How was it?"

"Fine. Go on and put your briefcase down, Dad. I'm going to go to bed. I am wiped."

He bobbed his head and went into his office. I hoped he'd at least take a break to eat and relax a bit tonight, instead of picking right back up working again.

I filled the next day with homework, wanting to get my English Lit assignment done so I could enjoy the rest of the weekend. It was a comparative essay on *Brave New World* and *The Hunger Games*, and it would not do to have it hanging over my head for the next three days.

~

I HAD a bounce in my step the first day back at school after the long weekend. On Saturday night, we got the play-by-play of Margaret's dance date with Xavier, including their first kiss. She was still so giddy, and it made me happy to see my friend all aflutter. On Monday, I put my headphones on and took a walk out to the falls, then returned home, built a cozy fire, and spent the rest of the day reading.

I had gotten my fill of solitude and was ready to return to society. As I walked into English Lit, I turned in my paper to the box on Mr. Zander's desk. Taking my seat, I looked up to see the guy I'd noticed at the dance walking into the classroom. His eyes swept the room before he turned and introduced himself to Mr. Zander, who pointed him to a seat near the door.

As the guy strode toward the desk, Mr. Zander began the class without mention of the new student. I tried hard to focus on the class discussion, but my eyes kept straying to the corner desk. I was lost in thought, trying to will his blue gaze to turn my way, hearing only the jumbled sound of tuned-out speaking.

"Celeste?"

Oh no. What did he just say? I tried to replay the last ten seconds in my mind, but all I got was something about a leather jacket. I was sure that wasn't Mr. Zander's question.

"I'm sorry?"

"Sorry for what, exactly?" Mr. Zander mocked me.

"I'm sorry I didn't hear the whole question. Could you please repeat it?" I gave him my best innocent look.

The teacher sighed at me. "Please explain the role of the utopian dream in *Brave New World*."

"Oh. Um. Well, Huxley uses the idea of utopia to extend our claimed ideals to their extremes and show that what we think is best for us will ultimately imprison us," I said, parroting the paper I had just turned in.

"Aha, and . . ." he said, running his finger down his clipboard, "Margaret, what does Ms. Atwood have to say about the dangers of taking our ideals to their extremes?"

I breathed a sigh of relief as my friend explained the premise of *The Handmaid's Tale*. I refocused back on the discussion in case I was called on again, which was all too likely to happen in our small class. I was glad when the bell finally rang, and began to put my notes away. When I looked up, the new guy had already slipped out the door and was gone.

"Are you studying in the library during tutorial today, Celeste?"

I turned to see Margaret putting her bag on her shoulder. "Yeah, I'll be there. Hey," I said, lowering my voice to a near whisper, "do you know who the new guy is?"

"New guy?" she repeated, looking around. "I don't see anyone new."

"He was sitting in the corner. You didn't see him come in?"

Margaret shook her curls. "No, I was trying to finish my Trig homework. I was a little busy this weekend . . ."

I chuckled. "A little busy making out with your new boyfriend, you mean?"

Pink infused Margaret's face. "Celeste!" She swatted me on the arm. "Well, maybe," she conceded. "He's so sweet, C, you don't understand . . ."

I tuned out as she babbled on about Xavier. She was right about one thing. I didn't understand. Boy-crazy was not in anyone's description of me, ever. But I'd be lying if I said the mystery of this new guy wasn't starting to drive me a little mad.

As we walked to our lockers, I scanned the hallway. He was nowhere to be seen, but Emma was coming our way in a hurry.

"Oh. My. God. You guys won't believe what just happened. Gary Smithson tried to pick a fight with the wrong guy. Come on!"

Margaret and I glanced at each other, then took off after Emma, who flew down the hall in front of us. We rounded the corner and saw a small circle of students surrounding two boys facing off. One of them was the mystery guy.

I gasped as Gary lunged at the taller boy, knocking the wind out of him with a shoulder to his middle. But tall, blond, and elusive was quick to recover, twisting to let Gary's forward momentum sail past him and straight into the lockers behind him. Gary rammed head-first into the lockers, and a trickle of blood ran down his forehead.

"Break it up," commanded Mr. Friske, striding purposefully around the corner. Students skittered away to avoid getting caught up in the principal's gaze, which was casting about for likely witnesses. My feet were sluggish, though, as Margaret tugged on my arm.

"Go on to class," I muttered to her, not even turning my head. My eyes were glued to the scene in front of me.

I saw her shrug out of the corner of my eye as she said, "Okay," and turned toward Ms. Wells's classroom.

Mr. Friske examined Gary's cut, then helped the bully to his feet and turned to face the new guy. "Mr. Burns," he said sternly, "I don't know how it was where you came from, but this type of behavior will not be tolerated in my school."

His only response was a cool stare.

"Go wait for me in my office while I take your sparring partner to the nurse."

"It wasn't his fault," I found myself piping up.

All eyes turned toward me.

"Did you see what happened here, Miss Long?" Mr. Friske asked.

"Uh, not all of it, but I heard that Gary started—"

"You heard, did you, Miss Long?" Mr. Friske cut me off. "Well, hearsay won't hold up in a court of law and it won't hold up in my determination either. Why don't you get to class before you earn yourself a tardy." It was not a question.

I turned to go, but not before I caught those bright blue eyes fixed on my face. I shivered and fast-walked to Bio lab, trying to dispel the blush crawling up my cheeks.

❧

JONATHAN

I WAITED in the principal's office while he took that bully to the nurse. This was exactly why I didn't want to come to this school. I preferred to mind my own business and for others to mind theirs. Having a jackass for a locker neighbor was not in my control.

"Well, Mr. Burns," the principal said, entering his office and closing the door behind him. "Let's start from the beginning, shall we? Tell me why you were fighting with Mr. Smithson."

"I wasn't fighting. I didn't throw a punch."

"Well, why were you there?" he asked. I was asking myself the same thing.

"My locker is there."

The principal picked up a folder from his desk, the same one that the secretary had leafed through this morning when she gave me my class schedule and locker combination. "Locker 246?"

"That's the one."

He pulled another page from his desk drawer. "And Mr. Smithson is at—" he ran his finger down the page—"247."

He looked up at me. I looked back.

"Did you say something to Mr. Smithson?"

Of course words were exchanged. But Friske didn't need to be apprised of them. I really didn't care what Jackass thought of my haircut. I shrugged. "I might have said hi."

Friske narrowed his eyes at me. "And how did he hurt his hand?"

"His punching form could use some work."

The principal raised an eyebrow. "So why aren't you the one in the nurse's office?"

I shrugged. "He didn't land many."

"Are you hurt?"

"It's nothing serious." Never mind that he *had* landed a few punches. My jaw would bruise, even though no one would see it, and my internal organs were still feeling the impact of that shoulder.

"Maybe you need to go see the nurse, too."

"I'm fine," I said. I had no desire to run into that buffoon again today.

The principal heaved a big sigh, as if I was keeping him from something important. "So how did he end up with his face cut?"

"He charged me." I shrugged again. "I moved."

Friske looked at me sideways, like he didn't believe a word of it. But he clearly didn't have anything on me, because he said, "As this is your first offense *and* your first day, I won't suspend you. Detention for the remainder of the week, and see the secretary for a new locker assignment."

"Yes, sir," I said, standing to leave.

"Mr. Burns," Friske said, stopping me as I headed for the door.

I turned back. "Yes?"

"Let's make this the last offense, shall we?"

"Yes, sir," I repeated, and got out of there before he ran out of stern looks.

∾

MAN, it sucked being the new kid. I didn't know my way around town yet, and most of the people I passed seemed friendly, but I could tell they were watching me like hawks. That's why I kept my guard up most of the time. Technically part of my glamour, it allowed me to go unnoticed by most people. It didn't exactly make me invisible, just created a sort of blind spot around me that it took extra attention to penetrate, unless you were right on top of me. Like Jackass was when he decided to pick a fight.

At least the place we were staying was close to the school, so I didn't have to walk through the center of town every day. Mrs. Walsh was living in the spacious house pretty much by herself, with her parents in a separate apartment over the garage, since her daughter Makenna had gone off to college. She was kind enough to take in my mom and me when we arrived less than two weeks ago, and I think she was glad for the company.

"Hi, Mom. Hi, Mrs. Walsh," I said, spying them in the kitchen sipping tea as I walked in the door.

"Jonathan," my mother said, "we need to talk."

Shit. She was mad. Of course the principal would have called her. I dropped my bag by the door and joined them at the high counter separating the kitchen from the dining room.

"How was your day?" she began, causing me to sigh inwardly. *I guess we'll be taking the long way around, then.*

"First day at a new school. I'm still trying to get my bearings."

"Did you make any friends?"

I glanced at Mrs. Walsh, who had turned and was pretending not to hear us as she rinsed off some dishes.

"It's all right," my mom reassured me. "Helena knows how we came to be here."

I nodded, continuing more quietly nonetheless, "No, I kept to myself, like you said."

"Then why did I get a call from Mr. Friske today about a fight?" she asked, anger creeping into her voice.

"Because the locker next to mine belonged to a bully," I snapped back. I was already tired of being blamed for shit that was not my fault.

Taken aback, my mom sat straighter on her stool and held my gaze for a long moment before taking another sip of tea and clearing her throat.

"I understand the other boy was injured, but not seriously. Did you hit him?"

"Not once, Mom. Defensive maneuvers only."

She nodded. "Okay. He's been suspended for two weeks."

"And my locker's been moved," I added.

"Good. Do you think you can steer clear of him after he comes back?"

"Yeah. He's a senior, so I don't think I have any classes with him."

She picked up her teacup and saucer and took them over to Mrs. Walsh at the sink. "All right. Let's go, then. I've made an appointment for you at the medical center."

What? "Why?"

"Mr. Friske suggested you get checked out, even though you said you weren't hurt."

"I'm fine."

"Okay. Let's go."

"A human doctor won't see anything, Mom. It's a waste of time."

"The doctor's not human. Next argument?" She picked up her car keys and walked toward the front door.

Rolling my eyes at my mother, I picked up my bag and followed her out the door, returning Mrs. Walsh's wave bidding us goodbye. I knew it was no good to argue with Mom once she had her mind made up. I was glad to see her acting like her old self again, though. The past month had been tough on both of us, and maybe getting used to life in a new town was just what we needed to distract us.

We had come to Havenwood Falls from another supposed haven, which proved to be not so secure, halfway around the world. It seemed no place was safe for us. The war raged on in Faerie, but its ramifications were felt in this world too. My father had fallen victim to it, but my mother was determined to keep us out of harm's way. I wasn't so sure that this new sanctuary was going to protect us, but it was probably as good a place as any to hide. We would just have to get better at hiding.

CHAPTER 3

CELESTE

*A*fter school, I walked across the street to my dad's office. I helped him out with filing and scanning a few times a week during the busy season so Polly, his office assistant, could concentrate on contacting clients and making sure all the deadlines were met.

"Hi, Polly," I said as I walked in.

"Hi, hon," she replied, looking up just long enough to smile before the phone started to ring. Her expression quickly flashed to annoyance before the smile returned so she could answer with a cheery "Long and Associates."

The space had three offices for accountants, though only two were occupied. The third office was half filled with boxes of old files and a desk with a computer and a scanner. That was where I worked, scanning receipts and other documents that clients brought in with their tax forms, and filing away originals we needed to keep.

My dad's door was shut, meaning he was in a meeting with a client, and the second office was dark. An independent accountant, Hunter James, rented the space from my dad and met with clients there, but he was seldom around.

I got to work and wasn't at it long before my dad knocked on the open door to get my attention. I turned, surprised to see he had someone with him.

"Hi, sweetie," he said. "Good day at school?"

"It was fine," I replied, keeping an eye on the man behind him.

"Good. I don't know if you've met Elsmed Fairchild before," he said, moving aside and gesturing to the man, who looked to be about a hundred years old, but stood upright in a suit and tie. "He was . . . a friend of your mother's."

"Oh," I said, a bit stunned. My mother did not often come up in conversation. "Hello."

The man's steely gaze seemed to chill me where I sat, and I shivered. "Good afternoon, Miss Long. May I have a few moments of your time?" Though he looked frail and walked with a cane, his voice was smooth and commanding.

"Of course, please come into my office," I tried to joke, but it came off empty as my growing unease made my voice shaky.

Unsmiling, he strode to the empty chair on the other side of the desk and sat, those eyes on me the whole time.

Polly came to the door and slipped a note to my father, probably letting him know a client was waiting on him.

"Excuse me, Mr. Fairchild, I've got to take this call. I'll be back in a few moments."

"No rush," said the old man. "I won't take too much of your daughter's time."

My father nodded and then abandoned me to this stranger.

I gave my best attempt at a smile, waiting for him to speak, because he clearly had an agenda.

"How are you doing, Miss Long?" he asked, making it sound less like a polite greeting and more like a therapist concerned about his patient.

"Fine?" I said hesitantly. *Who is this guy, and why is he asking me how I am?*

"As your father said, I knew your mother, and, well, her family, and I thought it was about time I checked in on you."

After fourteen years, he thought now *he needed to check on me?* "Oh. Well, I'm fine," I repeated. *Was this guy senile or something?*

His eyes seemed to flash a moment, and he heaved a sigh. "Any mood disturbances lately? Anything strange happen to you? Or around you?"

"Uh . . . no," I said slowly, not sure what he was getting at.

"And your father's been around? Not working too hard, is he?" the man asked.

What is this, an interrogation? "My father's around plenty," I snapped. "And in case you haven't noticed, I'm old enough to take care of myself." I'd had about enough of this weird guy and his weird questions.

He reared back, as if *I'd* said something to offend *him.* "Well, perhaps you should try keeping a lid on that temper, Miss Long," he had the nerve to say to me. "It won't go well for you if you continue to take it out on innocent people."

I felt my face flush instantly, whether from mortification or anger I wasn't sure. *Is he threatening me now? Who the hell is this guy to come in here and tell me how to act? He didn't even know me before today.*

"I've had my eye on you from afar for quite a while, Miss Long," he said, as if in answer to my unspoken question. "But your father has done an excellent job of caring for you, and I have not heretofore felt it was necessary to check on your well-being."

"But you feel it's necessary to do so now?" I retorted, trying to restrain the spitefulness from my voice.

"Well, as you pointed out yourself, you are nearly ready to strike out on your own," he said, adopting a conciliatory tone, like he was trying to soothe me. "I thought it wise to make sure you had everything you needed in the way of support."

Ha! This guy, supportive? I took a breath, about to give this old man a piece of my mind when my dad appeared back in the doorway.

"Sorry about that. I've been trying to get that client on the phone for weeks. Have you told her about the internship yet?"

My focus darted from my dad back to the old man. "Internship?"

"Ah, no, I was just getting to that." That piercing gaze settled on me again. "I came to see if you would be interested in interning for me. I would provide training, and you can help me with various errands that I need done."

"What kind of training?" I asked, too curious to reject the offer out of hand.

"Mr. Fairchild is a very important member of the community," my dad interjected. "He can teach you all sorts of leadership skills."

"What kind of errands?" I asked, letting suspicion creep into my voice.

He chuckled, though I wasn't sure what was so amusing. "Nothing too strenuous, I promise. I won't have you scrubbing floors or fetching coffee."

That wasn't much of an answer.

"My dad needs my help here," I began to decline this shady offer. "I couldn't leave him shorthanded during the busy season."

"Nonsense," said my father. "I've been thinking about hiring some part-time help for filing. You need to get some experience doing something more meaningful. Think of how it'll look on your college applications!"

I could see he'd already been sold on this idea. Filing *was* awfully boring. Maybe I could give this internship a chance, just to humor him. I could always quit if it wasn't my thing.

"Can you start tomorrow?" said Mr. Fairchild.

"I haven't said yes yet," I answered, then kicked myself mentally for admitting I was going to accept.

"Well, let's get on with it. I haven't got all day," he said.

I almost narrowed my eyes and glared at him, but I knew my dad respected this guy and would be upset if I lost my cool.

"I can start tomorrow, if you're sure you don't need me, Dad," I said, turning to my father again. He was practically beaming.

"No, no, she's all yours," he said, crushing my last hope of getting out of this bad idea.

Mr. Fairchild rapped his cane on the floor and rose. "Tomorrow, then. Meet me at City Hall after school."

Without waiting for a response, he walked toward the door, my father thanking him for the opportunity. I turned my back on them so they didn't see my massive eye-roll.

The next day, I trudged through the snow from the high school to City Hall after school. Mr. Fairchild was nowhere to be seen outside, so I went in the front door and looked around the large atrium. There were a few people bustling to and fro, but no old men with frosty stares.

I went to the security desk and asked a uniformed guard, who looked me up and down, as though wondering what I was doing asking after Mr. Fairchild. Finally, he said, "Down that hallway," pointed to a hall leading toward the back of the building, and turned away.

Raising my eyebrows at the curt response, I proceeded across the atrium and found a hallway with several offices for city and courthouse business. I walked past the Finance Department's office, the City Comptroller's office, and the Planning & Building Department's office before I found a series of doors bearing names, but no titles or departments. I came to a dark wood door with a frosted glass window pane that was embossed with the name Elsmed Fairchild in gold letters. I listened for a moment, but heard nothing. I couldn't tell whether anyone was in the office or not, try as I might to peer through the glass. I took a deep, steadying breath and knocked.

"Come in!" a distant voice called.

I turned the knob and stepped inside. There was a desk, though no one was sitting behind it, and some filing cabinets occupying the corners of the small room. Another entryway stood to my left, the door open.

"Mr. Fairchild?" I asked the empty space.

"In here," his voice called from the open doorway, and I stepped toward it. Elsmed sat behind a large desk piled high with papers and file folders, in front of which sat two upholstered chairs. Another more casual seating area off to the side contained a coffee table, more comfortable-looking furniture, and a buffet with a tea set on top. Along one wall were bookshelves filled with volumes, some looking new and some very, very old.

"Finally," he said as I approached. "Did you get lost on the way?" he began, darkening my mood.

"You neglected to mention exactly where your office was," I sniped, bringing that piercing gaze down on myself.

"Did I," he intoned. It was not a question, and I didn't answer, even as he gave me a long stare. "Sit down, please," he commanded, gesturing to the chairs in front of him.

I did as instructed and folded my hands in my lap as he considered me. *Why did my dad think this was a good idea?* I mentally rolled my eyes at my father. He really did care about me and tried his best to give me every opportunity, but sometimes his efforts were *so* misguided.

"Respect," Elsmed barked, startling me out of my internal rant.

"Respect?" I parroted, when he didn't seem inclined to continue.

"Respect," he repeated, "will be our first area of study. But first, let me make a few things clear. Nothing—and I mean *nothing*—that you observe during your internship with me may be disclosed to any other individual. Not your father, your best friend, your boyfriend, or even another person with an office in these halls. Do you understand?"

I nodded. "Complete confidentiality. Got it."

He studied me for another minute, then continued. "Second, do not allow anyone to accompany you to these offices. They are seldom visited, and I expect them to remain so. You may come and go for the purposes of your study with me, but at all other times, unless I have directed you to do so, there is no reason for you to be here. Clear?"

"Yes," I agreed. *I certainly don't intend to be here more than absolutely necessary.*

"Third," he said, "I do not have time to repeat myself or answer unnecessary questions. If I deem your questions relevant, I will answer them at the appropriate time. Is that clear?"

"Um, I guess so," I said with less certainty. *How am I supposed to know what he deems relevant? I don't even know what this internship is about. And what happens if I ask an "unnecessary" question? I guess he'll just ignore me? Seems pretty rude.*

"Now we can start on respect."

He lectured me for half an hour on the importance of respect. Respect for my elders, teachers, peers—basically everyone. He told me that courtesy begins within, and that I should always keep my thoughts civil, so that my words and actions would follow suit. I tried —really tried—not to roll my eyes, and I thought I did a pretty good job of keeping a straight face, but as he went on (and on and on) I felt like he was becoming angrier at me. Finally, he gave me a task to do.

"Take this stack of papers and put them in chronological order," he said. "While you work, practice keeping your thoughts respectful."

Stifling a sigh, I took the papers from him. *Great, more filing.*

"You can work at the desk out there," he said, gesturing toward the doorway, "but be sure to keep the area tidy."

"Yes, Mr. Fairchild," I replied, and took my pile of papers into the next room.

I looked at the first page. All it contained was a date. *Huh, must be a cover page,* I thought, flipping to the next one. That page had only a date as well. I paged through the stack quickly. Every page was completely blank, except for the date.

Feeling ready to explode with rage, I slammed the stack down on the desk. *Busy work? What the hell kind of internship was this?*

"Remember to focus on respectful thoughts," came the pompous voice from the old man's office.

Taking a deep breath, I tried to calm myself. Maybe it was just a mistake. Maybe he'd given me the wrong stack. Chiding myself for being so quick to anger, I stood, gathering the papers, and went back to Mr. Fairchild's office.

"I think there's a mistake," I said, making sure to keep my voice friendly. "All of these pages just have a date, and nothing else."

"It should be easy for you to put them in chronological order, then," he replied, his gaze fixed on the file open in front of him.

"Yes, but why—" I began, but stopped when his eyes cut to me.

"*Why* is not your concern, Miss Long. This task, while dull, needs to be completed. It should leave your mind disengaged enough to practice respectful thought. If you don't do it, I will have to. And I have more important matters to attend to. So if you don't mind . . ."

I do *mind,* I thought. *I didn't want to be here in the first place, and this is just a waste of time.* Unable to bring myself to say something nice, I turned my back and returned to the desk.

After a lot of internal grumbling and shuffling of pages, I settled into a rhythm. Just as I was about to crack a smile as I neared the end of my pile, Elsmed brought another stack of papers out and dropped it on the desk, saying only, "These too."

I only just managed to keep the pouting frown off my face as he shuffled back into his office. I decided that putting up a fight wasn't going to get me out of there any faster, and kept sorting pages.

After about two hours of the most boring internship known to man, there was a knock on the door, followed by a woman's voice. "Elsmed?"

Without waiting for a response, she entered, stopping short when she saw me. "Celeste?"

"Mrs. Augustine?" *What was Gianna's grandmother doing here?*

"What are you doing here?" she asked me, clearly as taken aback to find me there as I was to see her.

"Chronologizing?" I replied automatically, since I had just been debating with myself whether that was a real word. "I-I'm doing some work for Mr. Fairchild," I stammered.

"Are those Court records?" she said, her voice rising in pitch as if she had asked if the chair I was sitting in was on fire.

"Calm down, Mathilde. Of course not. She can't read them anyway," said Elsmed, coming through the doorway from his office.

Now it was my turn to be incredulous. "Can't read what?" I snapped. "They only have dates on them!"

"See?" he said, turning to Mrs. Augustine as if that answered all the questions. "Now, would you care to join me for a cup of tea?" He motioned for her to enter his office.

What the hell? My rage came barreling back, and I felt my face heating even as I somehow managed to keep my expression mild. I reminded myself that my dad would be very disappointed with me if I blew up at this geezer, so I'd better keep a lid on my temper.

Still obviously flustered, but at least somewhat appeased, Mrs. Augustine sighed, nodded, and went through the door, giving me a sideways glance.

"Almost finished?" he asked me.

I looked down at the last page, then quickly filed it in its spot and straightened the stack.

"Finished," I answered, mentally patting myself on the back for doing a fair job of keeping the anger out of my voice.

"Good," he said. "We are done for the day. Please come by again after your lessons on Friday."

I sighed with relief. At least I would have a break tomorrow from the never-ending pile of blank pages.

"Thank you, Mr. Fairchild," I said, though it almost physically pained me.

He gave me a tight smile.

"You're welcome, child," he said, before turning, following Mrs. Augustine into his office, and closing the door.

I got out of there and scurried home as fast as I could before the sun dipped behind the mountains.

CHAPTER 4

JONATHAN

I was used to small towns. Before coming to Havenwood Falls, we had been hiding out in a village in Portugal, surrounded by olive groves and vineyards. But even in the secluded countryside there, the hunters found us. When we heard a stranger on the road had been asking after us, my mother and I fled, escaping with only the clothes on our backs and the treasure my parents had been tasked with keeping safe. We later learned that our home had been burned to the ground that very day.

Before that, we'd lived in the highlands of Scotland, where my father had relied too heavily on his skills of concealment—the same skills I now possessed—and paid for that mistake with his life. It was only a matter of time before the hunters tracked us here; I was sure of it.

I had asked my mother if we shouldn't hide in a city—if it would be easier to remain anonymous among the crowds and noise. She said that it might be easier to remain hidden for a while, but that that very anonymity made it a dangerous place for hunted fae such as ourselves —our hunters could come and go as easily, and unnoticed, as we could.

So I looked over my shoulder often, kept my shields up, and used my enhanced glamour to make myself nearly invisible. This usually worked to keep us safe for a while.

I was used to small towns. But Havenwood Falls was *not* the average small town. It's hard to describe, but it felt like there was a delicate balance between the people here, as if one wrong step could throw everyone off kilter. I wondered if we'd stay long enough to assimilate into the town's population, or if we would be on the run again soon. My mom seemed to think that we'd finally found our safe haven. I was far more skeptical.

Being in detention for the fourth day in a row didn't bother me. I used the time to acquaint myself with the topics already covered in my assigned classes and with those yet to be covered. I found that, even though I had moved from school to school over the years, and they were generally small rural schools, I was already familiar with most of the material that had been covered. The only classes I was behind in were Government and English Literature.

I flipped through my Government book, keeping one eye on the other two students in the classroom and the teacher at the desk next to the whiteboard. She had been in and out of the room, clearly having more important things to do than babysit a few high school kids. Since the code of conduct was pretty strict, most serious infractions merited a suspension, and students in detention had done little more than arrive late for class or talk back to a teacher.

The aggressor who had landed me here was himself suspended for ten days, although I assumed he'd spend part of that time in recovery from his self-inflicted wounds. *Dumbass.* As far as I had heard, it was very rare to get off as easy as detention for being caught in a fight. I figured that somehow Mr. Friske was feeling charitable toward the new student, or he had concluded that I was blameless in the incident. I doubted it was the latter, so was busy pondering the likelihood of the former.

The teacher returned just as I glanced up at the clock. Only fifteen minutes left.

"Jonathan Burns? Is Jonathan here?" I heard her say when she got back to her desk.

Lowering my glamour's protection, I raised my hand. "Here," I said.

"A note for you," she said.

I strode to the front of the room to take it from her. As I did, she said more quietly, "You're excused for the rest of the day."

"Thanks," I said, opening the note as I went back to get my bag and books. It was from my mother, requesting that I meet her at City Hall on the town square. It went on to give directions to a particular office.

Pocketing the note and gathering my things, I raised my shield and slipped out the door.

City Hall was halfway across town, but I walked quickly and made it there in fairly short order. If we were going to stay here for any length of time, I needed to get some form of transportation. Passing by Havenwood Falls Garage & Tow, I noticed they had a few used cars for sale. I'd have to stop back and check them out when I had time.

I arrived at City Hall and found the office of Elsmed Fairchild, whom I'd met previously when my mom and I first arrived in town. He was apparently an old acquaintance of my parents. I knocked on the door with the elder fae's name on it, and stepped inside when I heard a faint, "Come in."

Closing the door behind me, I saw the girl sitting behind the desk, sorting through a stack of papers, and almost stumbled over my feet. The one who'd tried to save me from punishment earlier in the week, she was more than simply pretty, with delicate features, long wavy blond hair, and bright blue eyes that seemed to sparkle even in the dim fluorescent lighting.

"Hello," I said, keeping my cool.

She squeaked. Her mouth opened, as if she was trying to say

something, but no words came out. She just stared at me as if I had two heads.

Clearing my throat, I tried again. "I'm Jonathan Burns. I got a note to meet my mother here?"

Shaking herself to her senses, she blinked delicate lashes and nodded rapidly. "Yes, of course. Through there," she finally got out, pointing to a closed door on my left.

"Thanks." I nodded, reluctantly turning to knock on the second door.

"Celeste," she said, still staring at me, like she was waiting for something.

"Nice to meet you, Celeste," I responded with a smile, then opened the door and went inside to see what was so urgent it couldn't wait another fifteen minutes.

~

CELESTE

OH MY GOD. How much more of a fool could I possibly have made of myself? Did he ask you your name, Celeste? No. He didn't ask, and he doesn't care. And now he probably thinks you're an idiot.

I felt my face turn red, and just thanked my lucky stars no one else was there to see my humiliation. Shaking my head at myself, I continued putting pages in my stack. *Now at least I can put a name to that face, though.* I smiled to myself.

I wonder what he's doing here. Mathilde Augustine arrived a while ago, slightly less surprised to see me than she was two days before, followed a short time later by a middle-aged woman who introduced herself as Leah Burns.

I still had no idea what Elsmed Fairchild did, or what kind of internship this was supposed to be. My task for today was the same as the one earlier in the week, but today he lectured me on respectful speech, and told me to think on keeping my tone pleasant when speaking with others. I thought he just didn't like me talking back to him. *Ha! It's going to take more than a lecture and some paperwork to stop this mouth.*

~

"HAVE you noticed an unusual amount of strange occurrences around you?" Elsmed said. He had spoken with the Burnses for about half an hour before they left, looking very serious. I wondered what sort of business this new family in town could have with an elder statesman such as Elsmed. After they had gone, he asked me back into his office for a "chat."

"Strange how?" I asked. Havenwood Falls was its own brand of unique, according to my extensive research consisting of books and movies. I wasn't sure what qualified as strange in Elsmed's book.

"Have you felt you were able to influence the outcome of events without doing or saying anything?"

My brows wrinkled. *What a thing to ask.* Did he think I was some sort of weirdo that believed in telekinesis and other psychic powers?

"No," I said slowly, wondering where he was going with this.

"So you haven't noticed that things always seem to go your way, even when logically they shouldn't?"

"No. I don't think things always go my way at all." *Take this conversation, for example.*

The old man harrumphed. "What about other . . . turns of luck, shall we say?"

I thought for a minute, trying to decipher what he could be getting at, all while those piercing eyes were glaring at me. "I've been fortunate enough to witness the effects of karma recently, but that's about it." I sighed. "It restores my faith in the universe to see people get what they deserve."

I thought I saw Elsmed shiver suddenly. It was a bit chilly in the office.

"Karma," he repeated.

"Yes, karma," I said. "Like when the school bully rammed his own face into the lockers after picking a fight with the new kid. Oh, and the other day, this woman was being totally nasty to my friends and me, and the next thing we knew, she was tumbling down the mountain sideways." I shrugged. "I guess it could have been bad luck, or a coincidence, but I like to believe things happen for a reason."

"Oh, there's a reason," Elsmed muttered. He got up to pour a cup of tea, and the expression on his face was one I hadn't seen there before, like he was worried about something. "Listen, Celeste," he began, "there is a reason these 'karmic' things happen around you. It's not karma. It's you. You're doing it."

"Doing what?" I said, trying to understand what he was talking about. Maybe the old man really was starting to go senile.

"You're giving them a push, making them do what you want."

"A push? I never touched that woman on the slopes. She just fell. I was nowhere near her!"

Elsmed was shaking his head. "Not a physical push, a *mental* push. Your mind is very powerful, Celeste, and you can influence people without even realizing you're doing it."

Now it was my turn to shake my head. "That's crazy. How can I push people with my mind? Is this some kind of joke?"

"No joke, unfortunately. It's very serious. You have an innate ability to influence people's minds directly, sway them one way or the other at a moment of decision. We were able to overlook it until now, as you were a child and your powers were not fully developed. Now that you're becoming an adult, they are getting stronger, and you need to learn to control them."

I couldn't believe someone could spout this kind of nonsense and still be such a highly regarded figure in town. "So you're saying I have been controlling people, and now you want me to learn to control them better?"

"You need to learn to control *yourself*. To stop yourself from exerting that power you have over people. The mind is very vulnerable, and if you're not careful, you can do permanent damage. Abusing a power like yours is a grave offense."

"What, there are laws against mind control?" I scoffed. Fairchild was off his rocker, but I wanted to see how far he was going to take this foolishness.

"In this town, yes, there are."

I knew Havenwood Falls had some weird laws, but a mind control prohibition? That was beyond the realm of weird and into unbelievable.

"I would rather have waited to have this conversation with you, eased you into this idea, and given you time to adjust to it. But the truth is, it can't wait. You're a danger to others, and if you're not careful, Celeste, you won't just be doling out karma. You'll be facing your own. And you know what they say . . ."

"What's that, Mr. Fairchild?"

"Karma's a bitch."

CHAPTER 5

JONATHAN

*W*hat is it about small towns and their festivals? We had only been in Havenwood Falls for a few weeks, but it seemed like there was something going on every weekend. Last week, there was the Sweethearts Dance for Valentine's Day. I showed up, but I wasn't sure why, since I hadn't even been to school a single day yet.

Actually, I did know why. My mom. She insisted that it was important that I assimilate into the high school social scene, even though she kept reminding me to be careful who I made friends with. She was a bit conflicted.

This weekend, there was something called the Snowman Sled Races. I was too intrigued to stay away. My mom was huddled with Mrs. Walsh, doing some quilting or something.

Although it was at the other end of town, I walked there on my own, stopping in for a hot coffee at Coffee Haven about halfway there. Even though I'd lived in the mountains for the previous several years, Havenwood Falls was at a much higher altitude, and I sometimes became short of breath when walking around. As I got closer to Danzan Park, where the event was being held, I saw that plenty of other people were heading there, too. Almost all of them, from families with young children to older adults, dragged sleds behind them or carried one tucked under an arm.

I arrived to some kind of organized chaos. At the top of a gently sloping hill, people were milling about, walking around tiny plots of snow-covered ground that had been marked off with tape wound around stakes in the ground. At a table off to the side, they were handing out small cardboard signposts, which people were then taking to the plots to stake their claims.

There was a band playing on a small platform toward the back of the area, and tables set up with food and drink for sale. I approached the table where they were handing out stakes and picked up a flyer. "Snowman Sled Races," it read. "Claim your plot—Build a snowman —Race to win."

"Want to stake a claim?" a lady sitting behind the table asked, and I looked up, surprised to see she was talking to me.

"No, thanks," I replied. "Just here to watch. It's my first time."

"No problem, dear. There are some benches along the far side of the field where you'll have a great view of the races, but they aren't scheduled to start until two o'clock."

I nodded. It was only eleven thirty. I had thought I'd be fashionably late, but it looked like I was somewhat early for the spectator portion of the day.

I took my time strolling along behind the long plots, where people were scooping up the snow and forming it into balls.

"Jonathan!" I heard a female voice call. Looking around, I expected to see someone hailing a different Jonathan. It was a common name, after all. That was why my parents chose it. Instead, I saw the pretty girl from Elsmed's office making a beeline for me.

"Jonathan," she repeated. "Hey."

"Hey," I said. This wasn't awkward at all. "Celeste, right?"

"Right!" she beamed, obviously pleased I remembered her name. "Listen, I need your help. Are you racing a snowman?"

"No. No sled." I shrugged. "I was just going to watch."

"Perfect!" she cried. "Would you . . . I mean, if you wanted to . . . I need a partner," she finally got out in a rush.

"Oh, to help build?"

"Yes. I came with Margaret, Gianna, and Emma, but then Xavier came, and Margaret wants to pair up with him, which leaves me the odd woman out, so, well, if you wouldn't mind . . ."

"Sure," I said, seeing an expression of relief immediately brighten her face. "Lead the way."

I followed her to a little rectangular section of snow in the long row of plots. At the end of it was a rather slick-looking sled, painted pink and purple.

"Guys, this is Jonathan. He's going to help me with my snowman. Jonathan, this is Margaret and Xavier, and behind you are Gianna and Emma."

I waved at Celeste's friends, then looked down at our patch of snow. "So how big is this snowman we're building?" I asked.

"About man-sized," Celeste answered. "It has to be big enough to keep the momentum going all the way down the hill," she said, her cheeks already turning pink from the cold.

She pointed at what looked like some kids' beach toys—an assortment of pails and miniature shovels. "We can use those to scoop and pack the snow, so our fingers don't freeze off."

I grabbed a shovel and started scooping.

"So you're a junior too?" she asked, and I realized I'd just agreed to a two-hour interrogation.

"Yes." Maybe if I kept my answers short, I wouldn't have to reveal too much.

"When did you move to town?"

I doubted she really needed to ask. In a small town like this, everyone was sure to know when a new family arrived. Even a family as good at hiding as we were. "A few weeks ago."

"How do you like it so far?"

"It's okay." I could see the only way to stop the questions coming would be to go on the offensive. "How long have you lived here?" I asked.

"All my life," she said. "Never even been out of Colorado."

"Really? No family vacations driving across the country in a station wagon?"

That made her laugh. "No way. My dad is too tied to work to go away for more than a long weekend. And you watch too many movies."

I couldn't help my grin as I kept my eyes on the snow, scooping and dumping while Celeste formed the ice crystals into an ever-growing ball. "What does your dad do?"

"He's an accountant, has an office down in Miller's Plaza. How about yours?"

I stilled, taking a breath and letting it out. It still got to me after all this time.

"He's gone. Dead." I heard the wooden sound of my voice, followed by her small gasp.

"Oh, no. I'm so sorry. I didn't mean—" She looked into my eyes. "I didn't know. My mom, too. She passed when I was a baby." She took a step toward me and threw her arms around my shoulders. "I'm sorry."

The sudden show of affection stunned me, and I stood there like an idiot for a moment before I came to my senses and returned her hug. She was warm and smelled of cinnamon. "It's okay." We both turned back to our snow tasks.

"It must be hard to change schools in the middle of the year," she said, changing the subject. "Are you having an easy time catching up?"

"Mostly. I was living outside the country, so Government is the one I'm having the hardest time with."

"Oh yeah, I can imagine that would be difficult if you hadn't been raised here. I can help you if you want. I took it last year, and I still have all my notes."

"Thanks." I smiled. "That would be a big help."

"Where are you from, anyway? That accent is a bit . . . hard to place."

"Yeah, it's evolved over the years. Still a work in progress." I grinned, hoping to distract her from her prying.

She nudged me with a tiny shovel. "You didn't answer the question."

I chuckled at her persistence. I knew I wouldn't get off that easy. "We moved around a lot. I guess I picked up a little of the local accents all over Europe."

"I see . . ." she said, seeming lost in thought for several minutes while we silently worked side by side. We smoothed the surface of our snowman's bottom just as an announcer called out that there was one hour left for building.

"Are you copping a feel on our snowman?" Celeste asked, holding back a giggle.

"Who, me?" I put my most unbelievable innocent face on. "Nah, I'm more interested in the snow women," I smirked.

She let her giggle out now, turning a deep shade of pink. It was cute.

"You guys aren't going to finish on time if you keep standing there making eyes at each other," Emma said loudly from the plot next to us, flipping her light brown hair. I watched Celeste's expression turn from amused to decidedly not so, while her shade turned darker still. Neither one of us dignified the comment with a response, but got back to work and tried to ignore the giggles coming from Emma and Gianna.

After a few minutes, I noticed that Celeste was forming her snow into fist-sized balls instead of piling scoops onto the midsection of our snowman. I caught her eye and looked pointedly at the growing pile of snowballs, giving her an *Are you doing what I think you're doing?* eyebrow raise.

She replied with a *Yeah, what of it?* shrug, then added a *You in?* side-eye.

I responded with a *Hell yeah!* nod, and we quickly built up our arsenal of snowballs, hiding them behind the snowman's bottom, which we'd placed on top of the sled.

When we both silently agreed we had enough, I held up three fingers, turning down one, two, and then all three fingers. Celeste, crouched with snowballs in each hand, sprung up with a roar and started pelting Emma and Gianna. As much as I didn't like the idea of fighting against girls, when they started throwing snow back in our direction, I had to back up my teammate.

As we lobbed snowballs over the top of the giant half-built snowman and ducked for cover behind it, I noticed that revenge really brought out the best in Celeste. She was radiant, and I'd never seen a smile so big in my life.

"AND THE WINNERS ARE . . . Everett Weston and Graysin Ravenal!" shouted Mayor Stuart, whom Celeste had pointed out to me while we put the finishing touches on our snowman. He had hurtled down the hill behind the winning sled, then crumpled in a heap at the bottom of the hill, which was now a huge snowbank of wrecked snowmen with sleds sticking out.

"In second place, Jace Edwards and Zane!" I glanced over at Celeste, next to me. Her bottom lip was sticking out in a little pout.

"And in third place, Remy and Roxy MacKinnon! All winners please come up to the stage to claim your prizes!" We watched as they all filed up onto the little makeshift stage. Everett jumped as Graysin pinched his butt. This sent Emma and Gianna into a fit of giggles.

"Racers, collect your sleds. The hill is now open for sledding! Be careful, everyone." The mayor placed medals around the necks of the winners while racers began trudging down the hill to retrieve their sleds.

"I'll go get your sled, if you want to wait here," I offered.

"I'll go with you, man," Xavier said. He gave Margaret a peck on the cheek and turned down the hill. Celeste gave a brief nod and stepped over to put her head together with her friend.

I caught up with Xavier and fell into step beside him.

"Hey, nice job on your snowman today," I said. I'd never been good at making small talk.

Xavier laughed. "We barely finished it on time. We got a little . . . distracted."

I chuckled. I'd seen them stealing kisses when they thought no one was looking. "How long have you guys been together?"

"Just a week or so. I was so nervous she'd turn me down, I delayed four months before asking her out. Turns out she'd been waiting for me to ask."

"Sounds like you guys are meant to be," I said, almost choking on the platitude as it came out of my mouth.

He nodded and smiled. "I hope so, man. So what about you and Celeste?" he asked as we reached the sleds.

"Me and Celeste?" I said, surprised. I shook my head. "No, we're not together. She just needed a partner for the race."

"Dude, Celeste was bragging to us about how she'd out-build us on her own before you showed up. And I've never seen her blush so many times in one day. She's into you, man."

"Huh," I said, pulling out the purple-and-pink sled before brushing off the remains of the snowman and walking beside Xavier to the walkway with stairs leading back up the hill. "I don't really know her. I mean, we just met this week."

"Well, you may not know her, but it seems like you're into her a little, too," he said, looking pointedly at the sled tucked under my arm.

I didn't have a response to that, so I kept my mouth shut as we climbed back up the slope and made our way back to the girls. Celeste was certainly attractive and charming, but I'd never had the luxury of being able to fall for a girl. My life wasn't that of a normal teenager.

Mom and I were on the run, and I couldn't ever forget it. Couldn't let my guard down for a minute.

We'd been living in Portugal for three years before they found us, but when they did, we'd had to run and never look back. We would never be able to contact anyone there, for fear they'd trace us to our new location. How long would it be until Havenwood Falls was in our rearview mirror too, and we were looking for the next place to hide?

After a few sledding runs, we were all chilled and tired, ready to head somewhere warm.

"Napoli's for dinner?" Celeste proposed to the group.

"I'm in," Gianna said, dusting the snow off her sled.

Margaret and Xavier looked at each other and shared some kind of silent communication, after which Margaret announced, "Us too."

Five pairs of eyes turned to me. I froze. "Uh, sorry, I can't. Have to get home. My mom's expecting me for dinner."

Celeste's face fell a little, and I instantly felt guilty. Her words didn't betray a trace of feeling one way or the other, though. "Okay, well, thanks for being my snowman-building buddy."

"It was fun. Thanks for asking me to join." With a nod to Xavier and waves to the girls, I turned my back on the little group and began the long, cold walk home, mentally kicking myself the whole way.

It's best you don't form attachments here, I told myself. *You'll just have to break them sooner or later.* There were no hard feelings if you didn't have people to leave behind. There were no feelings at all.

CHAPTER 6

CELESTE

I was posing while Jonathan built a snow woman copy of me when a very loud and obnoxious horn started blaring just behind me. Actually, it was less like a horn, and more like—

My alarm clock. My eyelids fluttered open, and I rolled over to see an angry red 5:00 AM staring back at me. I silenced the assault on my ears and cursed Elsmed Fairchild.

He'd let me know before I left his office on Friday that he was signing me up for early morning Yoga in the Vines classes down at the Blackstone Winery on Tuesdays and Thursdays, for "training in meditation and mental focus techniques." I did not see how twisting my body into a pretzel was supposed to help my mental focus, not to mention doing it before I was meant to be awake on a school day, but he would hear no arguments.

When I appealed to my father about this ridiculous demand, he just said, "Yoga sounds like a great idea. You need to maintain your flexibility if you're going to keep skiing, you know. Just look at what happened to that tourist last week."

Thanks a lot, Dad.

I dragged myself out of the warm cocoon of my comforter and did the bare minimum to make myself presentable for a yoga class. I'd have to stop back home after the class to get ready for school.

If the alarm hadn't fully done its job of waking me up, the blast of freezing air when I opened the door to walk down to the winery certainly did. It was positively frigid, and the sun wasn't even up yet, though the sky was starting to lighten, coloring the wispy clouds in pastel purples and pinks.

While it hadn't snowed overnight, the sidewalks were icy, and it took a lot of attention just to keep from slipping and falling. With my head down, I picked my way around the slick patches and listened to the tree branches creaking under the weight of the ice that encased them.

This was probably the quietest I had ever heard the town. Even though it was small, Havenwood Falls never seemed to be completely quiet at night. There was often a rumble of motorcycles late at night, and people seemed to like going out for evening strolls after dinner, because I'd often hear footsteps outside long after dark.

One thing my dad was strict about, though, was my curfew. He really didn't want me out in the town at night. If I was safe in a friend's house, it was one thing, but I had to be inside by eleven o'clock. I wasn't sure what he was so worried about, but it was never a big deal, because most of my friends' parents were the same way.

I got to the winery and spotted a couple of ladies with yoga mats tucked under their arms heading for a cabin out in the vineyard. I had heard that Yoga in the Vines took place in the actual vineyard, but they cleared out one of the cabins to use as a yoga studio in the winter months. I followed them to the cabin, which had a sign on it reading, "Yoga in the Vines—Namaste."

I slipped inside and pushed the door shut behind me to keep the cold air out. There were a handful of ladies chatting as they put their shoes in cubbies and rolled out their mats.

"Namaste," said Letitia Blackstone, pressing her hands together and bowing slightly toward me. She looked to be about seventy years old, but was still limber enough to lead the yoga class. "It's nice to see a new face in class."

"Namaste," I responded, returning her bow. "I, um, don't have a yoga mat."

"Not to worry," she said, pointing toward the corner. "Just take a mat out of the bin there."

"Thank you," I said, and chose a mat, which I rolled out next to a beautiful woman with long wavy black hair, olive skin, and dark eyes.

"Hi," said the woman, "I'm Alina."

"Nice to meet you," I said. "Have you done this long? It's my first time."

"Oh, yoga? Yeah, I've had a few classes. Haven't got my poses perfect yet, but you can keep an eye on me, or Mrs. McCabe up there," she pointed to the woman in front of us, "if you need guidance. Letti doesn't do the poses herself, but she'll help you out, too."

I looked at Mrs. McCabe, who was flanked by Roxanne MacKinnon, a girl in my class at school, and Audrey Smith, Roxanne's older half-sister. Roxanne was super thin and had beautiful amber eyes. Her sister was more muscular and looked like she could be a dancer. All three moved with the grace of cats, and I guessed they had been doing yoga a while.

"Thanks," I said, feeling a little more at ease.

Alina turned to introduce herself to Sherry Grimes, who was setting up on the other side of her and eyeing the coffeepot in the back of the room.

Letitia put on some soft, nondescript music and started the class, reteaching us how to breathe for ten minutes before leading us through some simple poses that stretched my muscles and tested my balance.

"Beginners, please resume the child's pose. More advanced students, let's try the lord of the dance pose."

I curled myself in a ball and extended my arms the way Letitia had shown me earlier. The gentle stretch in my back became my focus as I breathed slowly and deeply, while she took the more advanced students through a few more poses.

"Everyone to easy seated pose."

I sat up slowly, tucking my feet in front of me, with my hands upturned on my knees.

"Close your eyes and focus internally," Letitia said as she walked around, straightening backs and nudging knees to get our positions right. "Listen to your breath," she said, pulling my shoulders back a fraction of an inch.

I closed my eyes and listened to my breath. I tried to tune out the other little noises in the room and the voice in my head reminding me of the assignments I had to turn in today. The darkness behind my eyelids was slowly emptying of afterimages and becoming deeper. The grainy colors disappeared until there were only a few points of light left. I counted them. Five stationary, and one that moved, floating above the others.

I watched the moving one and noticed its movements were not fluid, but it would circle around the others, stopping occasionally next to one or another. Curious. It stopped next to the point of light I estimated was closest to me, and I heard Letitia's voice nearby, speaking to Alina.

"Keep your back straight," she said.

I kept my eyes shut tight, focusing now on the remaining points of light that still wouldn't go away. As Letitia's footsteps moved on, the hovering point drifted away. Was my brain keeping placeholders for the people in the room? That would certainly be odd. I'd never noticed myself doing that before, but then again, I'd never tried any meditation techniques until then.

The hovering light came around again and stopped in front of me this time. I gazed at it, wondering what it would do next. As I did, it seemed to flash at me, just before a voice over my head said, "Chin down, Celeste."

My eyes burst open, and my easy seated pose fell apart. *Holy crap.* I looked up at Letitia, my jaw hanging open. She gave me a quizzical look.

"Something wrong, Celeste?"

I shook my head to buy time while I thought of something to say. Letitia glanced at the clock, then back at me.

"Savasana," she announced to the class, and I lay on my back, my mind racing. Did I really just *see* the minds of the other women in the room with me? I closed my eyes and tried to bring the vision back, but it was useless. My mind was full of unanswered questions.

What exactly was that, and was it real or something I just imagined? What if everything Elsmed had told me was true? If I could see people's minds, could I really influence them? How? And he said I'd done it before, but I'd never seen *that* before.

I couldn't process the words Letitia was saying, but I assumed they were supposed to be relaxing, wrapping up the session and giving us energy for the day ahead. All I could hear were the questions bouncing around my brain.

What was wrong with me?

"Namaste," Letitia said, and the other women started to stand up. I followed them in a daze as they rolled up their mats and put on their shoes and winter coats, readying themselves to brave the cold outside, except for Sherry, who made a beeline for the coffee machine.

"See you on Thursday?" Letitia asked me as I put my mat back in the corner bin.

I turned to her and nodded. "Definitely," I said.

Whatever I had just seen, I needed to know if it was a fluke or something I could repeat.

JONATHAN

I KEPT my head down on my way to school Tuesday morning. If I didn't make eye contact with anyone, my protective glamour had a better chance of staying intact. After I'd taken a seat in English Lit, a long pair of legs walked by my desk, and I looked up to see Celeste passing by on the way to her seat. I worried she'd seek me out, but she paid me no mind, going straight to her seat and plopping down, a dazed look on her face.

Fortunately, the class had started a new segment, so I was no longer behind on my reading and lost in the discussion. As Mr. Zander droned on about the use of imagery and its deeper meaning, I kept watch on Celeste out of the corner of my eye. She was clearly on another plane.

"So who can tell me what the use of the color white represents in this chapter?" Mr. Zander posed, casting about the room for a student to call on when, inevitably, no one volunteered to answer.

Almost in slow motion, I saw his gaze land on Celeste, a twinkle in his eye as he prepared to embarrass her for spacing out. Before I knew what was happening, my hand shot in the air, and I was proclaiming, "It represents purity and innocence."

Mr. Zander looked startled as his head whipped toward me, almost as though he'd forgotten I was in his class. With my glamour, he probably had. He paused a moment before nodding toward me and conceding, "Correct, Mr. Burns."

As he went on to direct everyone to open their books to examine a passage of the text, I saw Margaret smile at me in acknowledgment and nudge Celeste to bring her back from whatever planet she was currently inhabiting. Celeste gave her head a shake and turned to get her book out.

Clearly something had her preoccupied, and she had me preoccupied. I just wanted to reach over and smooth out that crease between her eyebrows. I didn't know her well enough to even guess at what might be bothering her, and that had suddenly become a problem for me. I knew I should keep my distance, but it was like I couldn't help myself.

When class was over, I watched for her to come out the door as I switched books at my locker, which had been moved to this hallway.

"Celeste!" I called to snag her attention as she floated by, still focused on something other than the hallway in front of her.

Her gaze jumped to mine. "Hey, Jonathan. How's it going?"

"Good. I just— You look a little distracted today. Everything okay?"

I watched the blush creep up her cheeks. "Oh, I'm . . . I'm fine," she said. "I just woke up early to go to this yoga class, and I'm a little tired, I guess."

"Tired."

"Yeah, you know, from lack of sleep?" she said, raising an eyebrow at me.

"Nah, I'm not buying it."

"Excuse me?"

"It's cool if you don't want to tell me what's bothering you, I get it." I leaned in toward her, holding her gaze. "Just don't lie to me."

Her jaw dropped, and a cute little gasp came out. The warning bell rang, and I closed my locker.

"Better get to class, Miss Long," I said in my best Mr. Friske impression, hauling my bag onto my shoulder. I hid my smile as she huffed and spun on her heel, then stomped off down the hall.

I headed in the opposite direction to French class, without an answer, but with an image of a blushing Celeste to keep me entertained for the next seventy-five minutes.

AFTER SCHOOL, I arrived home to find my mother frantic, and Mrs. Walsh's house in disarray.

"I don't know how this happened," she said, lifting the couch cushions and sliding her hands along the inside seams of the furniture, before turning the whole couch on its back to search the carpet where it had been sitting.

Mrs. Walsh appeared to be trying to stay clear while also preventing her house from being totally trashed.

"What's going on?" I asked, but neither of the women seemed to hear me.

"It's gone . . . It can't be gone!" my mother exclaimed, falling into a panic all over again and bringing her hands up to claw at her collarbone.

Oh shit. The pendant. The one thing we were supposed to protect, the whole reason we've had to hide for my entire life, was a pendant hanging from my mother's neck. It was there always, and I'd never seen her without it. Until now.

It was a tiny thing and looked like a gold filigree butterfly to most people—people who didn't look close enough to see it was a fairy. More than just a piece of jewelry, though, this was an ancient artifact of the Seelie fae. It had some mysterious power and was sent away from Faerie for safekeeping during the war. If the Unseelie got their hands on it, they could turn the tide against us, putting our people at risk.

It was given to my family to protect, and we had managed to do so for decades. My father's life had been sacrificed to keep this thing safe. Hell, my mother had never even wanted to tell me what the thing did, because she was so afraid I might let something slip that would lead our pursuers to us.

And now, in this supposed safest of safe havens, it had disappeared within weeks of our arrival. Never in my life had I seen my mother misplace the pendant. Could it have been taken? Had we been lured here under false pretenses? Or let our guards down too far?

My mind was spinning out of control, and I was about to lose my shit, when I heard a booming voice say, "Stop!"

Elsmed Fairchild strode out from the bedroom hallway, taking a cell phone from his ear and ending a call. "Everyone please take a seat and calm down, as best you can," he said, lowering his voice to a more reasonable level.

My mom and Mrs. Walsh righted the living room couch and sat on it, though I could see my mom still surreptitiously sticking her hands between the cushions to continue her search.

"The artifact is no longer in this house," Elsmed said.

My mom started sobbing.

Elsmed eyed her as he continued, "But it has not left Havenwood Falls. I can still sense its presence within our boundaries."

My mom's head shot up, renewed fire in her eyes. "Where? Can you tell where it is?"

"Not precisely," the elder fae answered. "Only that it's within about a five-mile radius. I've already alerted the Luna Coven to notify me of any movement across our wards. Why don't you tell us how this happened, Leah? Maybe that will give us a clue where to start looking."

"I was just reading here on the couch, and I guess I dozed off. I woke up, and it was gone."

"Do you often nap during the day?" Elsmed inquired. I looked at his face, but didn't see any traces of judgment there. My mother was still looking for work in this little village, but she wasn't anyone's definition of lazy.

"No, not really," my mom answered. "I don't even remember feeling tired."

"What else do you remember?" he asked.

Mom thought for a minute, her brows furrowed. "There was something . . . no, someone. I think?" She shook her head as if to clear it.

"I went out for some groceries," Mrs. Walsh said, "and she was in a panic when I came back. I was gone for less than an hour."

"Addie will be here any minute," Elsmed said, glancing at the door. "Perhaps she can help clear your mind."

I helped Mrs. Walsh put away her groceries while my mother

paced and Elsmed glared at the door. After a few minutes, a knock at the door announced a young woman with long brown hair, black-framed glasses, and a diamond piercing in her nose. I recognized her as Addie Beaumont, the witch who had given us tattoos as part of the town's registry process when we first arrived.

"It's about time," Elsmed said, casting a stern look at the newcomer.

She ignored his comment. "How can I help?"

"Mrs. Burns has had something of great value stolen from her person, but she doesn't recall the incident," Elsmed explained. "Could you please see if she has a memory block and remove it?"

"Of course." Addie smiled, turning to my mom. "Let's have a seat, and we can get started." She led my mom to an armchair beside the couch. "Now just close your eyes and try to relax," she said.

My mother closed her eyes and took a few deep breaths while Addie stood in front of her and began chanting in a low voice. After a minute, she stopped and nodded to Elsmed.

"What happened after Helena went to the store?" Elsmed inquired.

"I-I was here in the living room, reading the paper. There was a knock at the door. I looked out the window and saw a woman with . . ."

"Take your time," said the older fae in a surprisingly gentle voice.

"Sorry, it's still a bit fuzzy. She was holding something—a potted plant or . . . a flower arrangement? I remember thinking it looked unwieldy, so I opened the door and stepped outside to help."

"What did the woman look like?"

"She had fair skin, dark hair—I can't quite get a grasp on her features," my mother said, frustration creeping into her voice.

"What happened when you opened the door?" Elsmed continued.

"She shoved the plant at me and said something I didn't understand. It might have been Latin? I don't remember the words now. After that . . . I don't remember anything before I woke up on the couch, when Helena came back."

"Hmm. She must have knocked you out. Was there anyone else with her?"

My mom thought a moment and shook her head. "I don't think so."

"It was definitely a witch's spell on her mind," Addie volunteered.

"All right," Elsmed said. "I want immediate reports on anyone crossing the town borders. You and Saundra should take account of any members of the Luna Coven matching the description, and I'll talk to the sheriff about setting up surveillance on the other witches in town."

"Wow, it's a literal witch hunt," I heard myself mutter.

Elsmed's cold eyes swung to me. "You didn't tell anyone about the pendant, did you, boy?"

"Of course not," I answered.

"Good," he said. "I want you to stay with your mother until this is all sorted out. Make sure there are no aftereffects of the spells. If you see anything out of the ordinary, call me or Addie. Helena has our numbers."

"We'll call Mr. Friske," Mrs. Walsh added, "and let him know your mom is keeping you out of school for the time being. Maybe your teachers can put together some assignments for you so you don't fall behind."

I doubted that would be necessary, but didn't contradict her; she was just trying to help. I was fairly sure we'd be leaving town once we tracked down the pendant, whether it took a day or five weeks.

We all wanted to get on with the search, so Elsmed and Addie left. Mrs. Walsh tried to distract my mom by enlisting her help with dinner preparation.

I wanted nothing more than to be out there hunting down the perpetrator of this theft, but knew there was not much I could do with the little knowledge I had of the town and its residents. I set up camp in the living room and tried to focus on my homework.

CHAPTER 7

CELESTE

I wandered through my day in a haze. There had to be a rational explanation for what I had seen. Maybe my mind was playing tricks on me. I woke up too early, and the lack of sleep was messing with me. I came up with a dozen explanations, but none of them seemed to ring true. Instead, over and over, my mind kept repeating Elsmed's words back to me.

"You have an innate ability . . ." *Ridiculous. If I had an innate ability, wouldn't I have noticed it by now?*

". . . to influence people's minds directly . . ." *If that were true, I would have everything I ever wanted. Was this his way of saying I'm spoiled?*

"We were able to overlook it until now . . ." *Come to think of it, my dad is kind of a pushover. But that's not my fault, is it?*

". . . your powers were not fully developed . . ." *So maybe that's why no one noticed before? Has anyone noticed now? Besides Elsmed, of course.*

". . . they are getting stronger, and you need to learn to control them . . ." *What will happen to me if I can't? Will I go to mind control jail?*

I shook my head. This just sounded crazy. Maybe Elsmed was just an old kook who got his kicks tormenting teenage girls. *I should talk to Dad and get myself out of this weird internship.* Then I imagined the look on his face when I told him I didn't want to continue. He would be disappointed. Tell me he only wanted the best for his little girl. *Ugh.* Who was the controlling one after all? For that matter, he'd think *I* was the crazy one if I told him I thought I had some psychic power. I didn't think I could endure the therapy he would surely insist upon if *that* came out. Better to just suffer through a month or two with Elsmed.

Still, I kept coming up with new questions, all of them unanswered. Where did this ability come from? Why me? Was I the only one? Did my dad have any idea about this? Did he have abilities himself? What about my mom? Or was there a radioactive spider to blame? I turned the questions over and over in my head, going through the motions at school and walking home on autopilot. I vaguely registered Margaret trying to flag me down as I headed for the main door of school, but it was like I was stuck on a track, unable to deviate from my path or turn my eyes toward her, just as I was unable to turn my mind from its problem.

Once home, I took out my books to study, but no amount of staring at them and turning pages could help me concentrate on what was in them. Instead, I sat cross-legged on my bedroom floor, closed my eyes, and focused on my breathing.

My dad was still at work, and the house was empty. I saw nothing but darkness behind my eyelids. I waited, clearing my mind of any thoughts that popped into it. I concentrated on the in and out of my breath, the filling and emptying of my lungs. I waited.

I don't know how long I sat there like that, focused inward, before I saw a tiny light, like a faraway star. It floated down below me, from far away, but coming closer. I watched as it bobbed along, moving more or less in a straight line, slowing as it approached. It came to a stop nearby. If I'd pointed myself directly at it and opened my eyes, I'd be looking at the sidewalk in front of my house.

But I didn't dare open my eyes. I watched as it floated there for a moment, then made a right turn and moved a little closer. It paused again. I held my breath.

Ding-dong!

I won't lie, I screamed a little. My doorbell had me almost jumping out of my skin. "Oh my god." I got to my feet and raced down the stairs, my heart pounding in my chest. "Oh my god, oh my god, oh my god." I peeked through the peephole and saw Margaret fidgeting on my doorstep. I opened the door and greeted her with "Oh my god."

"Celeste?" She looked surprised, and a bit worried. I waved her inside, looking up and down the street behind her. Empty.

"Oh my god, Margaret. You are not going to believe this."

"What's up?" she asked, definitely confused now.

I closed the door behind her and lowered my voice, though no one was around to hear us. "I *saw* you coming."

"Uhhh . . . okay," she said slowly.

"But not with my eyes," I said, watching the look of confusion grow on her face. "With . . . my mind." I shook my head. "It sounds so stupid when I say it like that."

"Why don't you start from the beginning?" she said, taking my hand and leading me to the sofa. She thought I was going crazy. I thought I was going a little crazy too.

"Okay," I began. "So I was meditating—"

"Wait, what?" she interrupted. "When did you start meditating?"

"This morning." Her eyebrows rose. I pressed on. "So I was meditating, and I saw you coming closer, and then you rang my doorbell."

"Like a vision?"

"No, it was like a little light."

"Uh-huh." She looked at me expectantly, waiting for more.

"And it happened this morning, too."

"You saw me this morning?"

"No, I saw the other people in my yoga class."

"And where were you?"

"In my yoga class. But with my eyes closed."

"I see. And when did you start taking yoga?"

"This morning."

"So let me get this straight. This morning you started a yoga class, learned to meditate, and started seeing—"

"Lights."

"Lights that you think are people—"

"I think maybe it's like a representation of other minds? Like their consciousness?"

"Uh huh. So you see other people's minds when you close your eyes."

"Just if I'm concentrating. And I think they have to be close to me. Or maybe it only works if I know them? I don't know, but I don't see a lot, only a few. Or one, just now."

She still had a look of disbelief on her face. "Are you sure it's not your imagination? Or, I don't know, a hallucination?"

"Did you tell me you were coming over here today?"

"No, I just saw you in school looking like a zombie, and decided to check on you. Maybe it's lack of sleep?"

"When you came over just now, you stopped—hesitated—on the sidewalk before coming to the door."

Her eyes shot to mine. "Yeah."

"I saw that."

"With your eyes closed."

"With my eyes closed."

"Did you know it was me?"

"Not until I got to the door."

"Huh."

I just nodded. I could see she was starting to believe.

"So is this why you were a zombie today?"

"Yeah, I guess. I kind of can't stop thinking about it."

"Hey, I don't blame you. If I had a superpower, I'd be a little zoned out at school, too," she said.

"It's not exactly a superpower," I said.

"So what is it, exactly?"

"I'm not sure." I shrugged. I wanted to tell her about what Elsmed had told me, about an ability to not only see minds, but to influence them. But I remembered his warning about keeping our chats between us, and I had a feeling I did *not* want to piss him off. "I just need to get my mind off it, or I think I'll go crazy wondering what it is, and where it came from."

"Okay. Want to study for the history quiz?"

I grinned. Margaret really was the best kind of friend. "Absolutely."

THE NEXT DAY, I had regained my focus. As I sat in my morning math class, I started a list of questions for my new mentor. *How does this mind control thing work? Are the lights I see really other people's minds? Is that vision related to the power to influence? Why do I have to meditate to see the lights?*

So many questions. I wondered how many of them I'd actually get answers to. Ms. Wells was talking about logarithmic functions, and I wondered if I could put myself into a meditative state with her droning as background. She really didn't like people sleeping in her class, though, so I thought I'd better not test it.

I looked around surreptitiously for Jonathan. I had spotted him in this class before, though he often snuck in somehow without my noticing. I didn't see him. I started paying attention and taking more detailed notes. It never hurt to have good notes. And if a certain someone who, say, missed class asked for them later, then I'd be able to help him out.

During my last class of the day, the office sent a note saying I should meet Mr. Fairchild at an address in Creekwood Estates after school let out. My mind started going in circles again, wondering what was up with the change in venue, and what he had planned for me today. I was fairly certain it wouldn't be paperwork, and for that I was grateful and excited.

When the final bell rang, I headed straight for Creekwood Estates and found myself standing in front of a house with the address matching the one on my paper. I approached and knocked on the door, then I thought I heard scurrying before Elsmed's voice came through, saying, "It's all right. It's just Celeste."

Elsmed opened the door. "Good afternoon, Celeste."

"Good afternoon, Mr. Fairchild."

"Please come in."

I stepped into the house and looked around. A woman I recognized as Mrs. Walsh, Makenna's mom, was standing in the kitchen, with one hand resting nonchalantly next to the knife block. Makenna was a couple years ahead of me in school, but in a small town like ours, it seemed like everyone knew everyone else, at least superficially. Mrs. Burns, whom I'd met in Elsmed's office the other day, was standing in the living room behind Jonathan, who was looking quizzically at me. In fact, they were all staring at me, as if waiting for me to sprout wings or something.

"Hi," I said meekly, giving the room a little wave of my hand.

The women seemed to relax a bit, and Jonathan waved back at me. "Hey."

"Have a seat, Celeste," Elsmed said. "There's a lot to fill you in on."

I sat on the edge of the armchair he gestured at. "O-okay." *Fill me in? Yeah, 'cause I've got no clue what's going on here.*

"You are—" He paused, shook his head, and started again. "We need your help."

"What kind of help?"

"Mrs. Burns has been robbed."

I gasped. "Oh, no! Are you okay?" I automatically asked.

She just shook her head, looking like she was unable to speak.

"We need to keep her safe until we track down the perpetrator," Elsmed continued, bringing my attention back to him.

I felt my brows crinkle together. "Safe?"

"Yes, it seems that the . . . artifact that was stolen has a . . . key of sorts, and we expect the thief will be back once he or she figures that out."

My eyebrows tried to climb up my scalp. "Oh. I haven't . . . I mean, I'm not that strong, and I wouldn't know how— I'm no bodyguard, Mr. Fairchild. How can I help?"

"You remember that gift we talked about before? Your mental ability?"

Uh, yeah. How could I forget? I nodded.

"I hope you don't mind, but I discussed it with Mrs. Burns and Mrs. Walsh, and we agreed it would be very useful for keeping away unwanted visitors that might be a threat. I need you to turn away anyone who tries to approach the house. Everyone but those of us here and Addie Beaumont."

Now my head was shaking of its own accord. "Not possible. I don't know how to do that."

"You do. You've just never done it consciously before. Try it."

I looked at Elsmed. *Go upstairs*, I thought at him, focusing all my willpower.

"It won't work on me," he said with a chuckle. "Try someone else."

I rolled my eyes. "I *told* you I can't."

"Try again," he said sternly, those steely blue eyes growing even colder.

I looked around the room, my gaze settling on Mrs. Walsh, who was staring at something on the kitchen counter, pretending not to listen to our conversation. *Pick up a pencil*, I mentally commanded her.

She looked up at the bulletin board hanging on the wall and reached up to grab a pencil that was balanced on the top of the frame.

My eyes went wide.

Put it behind your ear, I silently told her. She did.

"What the—"

"Watch your language," Mrs. Walsh called absentmindedly, as if she was used to scolding a child.

I looked at Elsmed in wonder. "How?" was all I could manage.

"That is a question I do not have time to answer right now, unfortunately," he sighed. "I have to go speak to a potential witness. Time is of the essence in this matter."

"Wait, what if . . . what if it doesn't work?" I asked, nervous to be entrusted with this responsibility.

"If there is any problem, call me." *With your mind*, I heard his voice add in my head.

I shrieked, my eyes going wider than I thought they could. "What was that?" I squeaked.

"A reliable communication system, better than cell phones," he answered with a rueful smile. "Call if you run into any problems. Stay here, all of you," he broadened his address to the room. "Jonathan's been on guard all night and day, and he needs a rest."

So that's why he was nowhere to be seen at school today.

"I have questions," I said. *Even more now than before.*

"And I will answer them, later," he said. "I really must be on my way now. Call your dad and let him know I'll be keeping you late, but you'll be home before curfew."

I nodded again, too overwhelmed to say anything.

He waved to Mrs. Walsh and Mrs. Burns, then disappeared out the door. Mrs. Walsh hurried over to lock it behind him.

I looked from Mrs. Walsh to Mrs. Burns, not sure what to do or say.

"My, you look terrified, darling," Mrs. Walsh began, and reached out her hand to me. I took it, and she led me to the kitchen. "How about a hot cocoa?"

Polite Celeste kicked in. "Thank you, Mrs. Walsh, that would be lovely."

She started some milk heating on the stove.

"Jonathan, honey, why don't you head up to bed?" Mrs. Burns said quietly to her son. "Celeste will watch over us while you get some sleep."

Jonathan studied me as if seeing me for the first time. It seemed like maybe he didn't trust me, or wondered about my capability to keep his mother safe. I didn't blame him. I wasn't all that confident in myself as a security measure, either. But Elsmed must have had a good reason to choose me for this task, I supposed. I would try my best. Jonathan finally nodded his head and trudged up the stairs to take a nap.

Mrs. Walsh and I pulled an armchair from the living room to a spot right in front of the window facing out onto the street. From there, I could see anyone approaching the house from the front.

"Now you just sit right here," Mrs. Walsh said, pulling the curtains back to give me a good view of the street, "and I'll get your cocoa."

"Thank you, Mrs. Walsh," I said, and made a quick call to my father, letting him know I'd be home a little late.

After a few minutes of fussing in the kitchen, she brought me a steaming mug topped with marshmallows. There were even a couple of cookies on the saucer.

"You are too kind," I said.

"Nonsense," she replied. "You're the one doing us a favor."

I smiled and took a sip of my cocoa. "Delicious."

"Okay, I'm going to take my knitting and go keep an eye on the back of the house. If you need anything, I'll just be straight down that hall in the sunroom." She pointed toward the back of the house.

"Okay." I nodded.

"Don't you worry," she called as she made her way down the hall. "Elsmed will be back before you know it."

I settled into the chair and stared out the window, afraid to take my eyes off the street. Since Creekwood Estates was a residential development, there wasn't a lot of activity out there, and I wondered how long it would be before I dozed off.

Mrs. Burns pulled up a chair across from me, out of sight from the window. "Thank you for doing this, dear," she said. "I'm afraid we're all a bit shaken up."

I gave her a warm smile. "It's no problem."

"So, do you know my Jonathan?"

"Yes, we have a few classes together, and we hung out on Saturday, at the Snowman Sled Races."

"Oh, yes, he told me that was fun. Thank you for making him feel welcome."

I shrugged, turning my head to hide my blush. "He's cool."

We both sipped our drinks and sat in silence for a few moments before Mrs. Burns said, "Tell me about your family, Celeste."

"Oh, it's just my dad and me. He's an accountant; he does the books for a lot of the businesses in town. My mom died when I was little. I don't really remember her."

She nodded. "We lost Jonathan's father some years ago now, but Jonathan was old enough to remember him, and miss him." She started to tear up.

"I'm so sorry," I said, keeping my eyes fixed on the street so she could regain her composure. "Jonathan said you moved around Europe a lot, but your accent is different from his." I tried to change the subject.

"Yes, well, Jonathan's lived here his whole life, but I grew up in Faerie, and lived there many years before coming here."

"Faerie?" I shook my head. "Where is that?"

"Why, it's our homeland, dear. Has no one ever told you about it?"

"N-no . . ."

She clicked her tongue. "You're young yet, and there's been so much turmoil, I'm not surprised you haven't been, but I would have thought you'd at least heard of it." She had a perplexed look on her face. "Faerie is where our people come from. My family, yours"—she considered me—"or at least one of your parents, the Walshes, the Fairchilds. All the fae."

"Fae?" This woman was making less and less sense the more she talked.

She looked at me as if I were the crazy one. "Yes, of course. Fae come from Faerie. Did you think we were native to the earth realm?"

"Uh, yes. Are you saying you—we—are some sort of aliens? Is that why I have this ability?"

"In a way, I suppose you could say that," she said, tilting her head. "You didn't know?"

"No, this is all news to me. As far as anyone ever told me, I'm human. My dad's human. I thought everyone in this town was human, but you're telling me there's an alien—fae—population living here too?"

"Oh, there's a lot more than fae and humans in this town. There are shifters—humans that turn into animals—vampires, angels, demons, witches . . . Well, you don't need the complete list. Suffice it to say there are a number of supernatural species in town, and all living side by side." She shook her head. "It's amazing, really."

Vampires? Demons? People who turn into animals? This was insanity. I looked at Mrs. Burns again, but she didn't seem as though she were joking or trying to trick me.

"How do you know all this? Didn't you just move here?"

"Oh, yes, dear. But that's my ability—species identification. I can tell by looking at a person what they are, even if it's hidden from human eyes."

I turned my attention back to the window, trying to process what she'd told me. I would ordinarily think she was off her rocker, but this did give me an explanation for what was happening to me. Was it possible I'd been in the dark my whole life about not just who I was, but *what* I was?

"So is my dad fae too, then?"

"I'm not sure; I'd have to meet him. You definitely are, but you're also a bit human, so he could be human, if your mom was fae."

"Why didn't he tell me?" I said aloud, though really I was talking to myself.

"Maybe he was waiting until you were older. Or if he is human, maybe his memory was altered. They seem to be pretty strict in this town about keeping humans in the dark." She seemed to realize something, her face draining of color. "Oh, my. I think maybe . . . I shouldn't have said anything to you. I was warned not to speak of supernatural affairs to humans, but, well, you aren't human, are you?"

I shrugged. I didn't know what I was anymore. "Don't worry, I won't tell. Does Jonathan know?"

"He knows about you, just because of your position. Elsmed is an elder of our people, and he would not likely be mentoring you unless you were fae as well. And Elsmed did tell us about your ability, as it's pertinent to our security situation. It's so kind of you to help us like this. We have been running for a long time, but I didn't imagine they'd catch up to us again so quickly, not here."

I nodded, even though I had no idea what she was talking about. Why were they on the run? Had she done something wrong? Had Jonathan? Questions were bouncing around in my head so fast, I almost didn't notice the teenage boy on the sidewalk, eyeing the house as his steps slowed. I did a double take and recognized him as Remy MacKinnon, a boy I knew from school, though he had only moved to town a few months ago.

I focused on him, tuning out everything else jumbling my mind. *Go away*, I commanded him with my mind. *Keep on walking.*

His steps picked back up, still slow, but he was moving. *Go home*, I directed him, putting every ounce of my willpower into pushing that idea on him. *You have to be home, you have to be there now, and there is nothing here to stop you.* His head turned away, looking across the street as he passed the Walsh property and picked up his pace again.

I heaved a sigh of relief.

CHAPTER 8

CELESTE

*R*emy was back. He came from the other direction now, from what I guessed was his home, somewhere here in Creekwood. About an hour had passed since his first pass by the house, and this time he was headed straight for it.

"Go upstairs and call Elsmed," I said to Mrs. Burns, before calling out to him myself. *Help!* was all I could manage before turning my mind to pushing this boy away. I heard Mrs. Burns running up the stairs.

Turn around and run, I commanded him. He seemed unfazed, crossing the street diagonally. *You need to be at Danzan Park,* I pushed on him. *You're meeting someone there.* He didn't even flinch.

Just as he approached the front porch, I heard a woman's voice behind me. "What's going on?"

I turned to see Addie Beaumont standing in the living room, looking around at the empty space. *How did she get in here?* I pointed to the front door. "Someone is here. I couldn't turn him away."

She nodded her understanding as a knock sounded on the door. "Stay out of sight."

I tucked myself behind the wall next to the stairs while Addie answered the door.

"Hello, can I help you?"

"Uh . . . is this the Walsh residence?"

"Yes. How can I help you?"

"I-Is Mrs. Burns here?" he stammered. "I have a . . . message for her."

"I'll take it," Addie replied.

"No, I have to give it to her personally," the boy said.

"No, you don't." Addie's tone said she was brooking no argument.

"If she's out, I can wait—"

"Oh, to hell with this," Addie muttered before she unleashed a string of what sounded like Latin. After a moment, she called, "You can come out, Celeste."

I came back into the living room to see Remy looking straight ahead, vacantly, while Addie pushed him into a chair. "Watch him, but he should stay put for a while. I'm going to call someone to come pick him up," she said, then went into the kitchen to use the phone.

I moved to the front window again, keeping one eye on the street outside the house, and one on the boy in the chair. He didn't even blink; it was as if he were sleeping with his eyes open. Creepy. I also saw he was wearing a jagged black stone on a leather cord around his neck. I wondered if that could be the reason my pushes didn't work on him.

Addie finished her calls and proceeded to start pulling things out of her messenger bag—candles, jars, and bundles of herbs.

"I'm going to refresh the wards on the house," she told me. "Help should be arriving momentarily."

After a few minutes, I saw Elsmed arrive out front, at the same time as Mike McCabe. They shook hands and exchanged a few words, then approached the house and opened the front door without knocking. Surveying the living room with a frown, Elsmed finally settled his gaze on me.

"Celeste, thank you for your help. I'll cover the front door. Why don't you go and check on Mrs. Walsh and Mrs. Burns?"

I nodded and proceeded to the sunroom to fill Mrs. Walsh in on what had been occurring in her house since she'd left us. I arrived in the bright, chilly room to find Mrs. Walsh slumped over in her chair, eyes closed, her knitting fallen to the floor.

"Mrs. Walsh," I exclaimed, running over to her. "Are you okay?" I shook her shoulder gently, but she didn't wake up. Quickly checking her pulse, like we'd learned in health class, I found it steady and strong.

But I was sure Mrs. Walsh hadn't just passed out for no reason. I scanned the room, and my gaze snagged on the side door—unlatched. Otherwise, though, the room was empty and undisturbed.

If someone had taken out Mrs. Walsh, it was likely they were still in the house. Instead of yelling for help, I crept noiselessly back to where Addie was chanting over a crystal in the corner and told her what I'd found.

She gestured for me to follow her up the stairs. I did, trying to make as little noise as possible. When we reached the top landing, we heard muted voices coming from behind a closed door. To the left, the hallway led to a bathroom and a bedroom, both with open doors. To the right were two closed doors and one open doorway nearer the stairs.

"Let him go!" we heard Mrs. Burns cry.

"Give me the key, and he's all yours," said another woman's voice; I didn't recognize it. Addie pointed at the nearest closed door, and I slunk along behind her as we approached it.

"You're not even fae! What could you possibly want the key for?" Mrs. Burns stalled.

"It's not for me, you idiot; it's for the Collector. And I don't care why. All I ask is how much I'm getting paid." This brought Addie up short, and she cocked her head as if confused.

"And how much is that?" Mrs. Burns asked.

The woman laughed. "Much more than you could ever hope to scrape together, if you're thinking you can outbid on this job."

I peered in through the open doorway as we passed it; it looked like Mrs. Walsh's bedroom.

"Please, just put down the knife, and we can talk about this."

A knife! Fear crawled up my throat, and I pushed it back down. If we lost the element of surprise, it could be disastrous for Jonathan and his mom. I put a hand on Addie's shoulder, tilted my head toward the open bedroom, then tiptoed in. She stayed in the hall.

"There's nothing to talk about. Give me the key, or I'll slice this boy's throat. Even your kind don't heal that quickly," the intruder sneered.

I dropped to a seated pose on the plush beige carpet and closed my eyes, trying to tune out her threatening words. With all the tension, I was afraid I wouldn't be able to bring myself to a meditative state. My mind raced, and my heartbeat thundered in my ears.

"You'll never get away," Mrs. Burns said.

I tried to focus my mind, but it felt like a whirlwind of emotion. I put my hands in my lap, palms together, and imagined the whirlwind as a tangible thing. Once I saw it in my mind, I tilted the funnel cloud out slowly, pushing it until the center pointed away from me. I took a deep breath and blew out slowly, releasing the whirlwind as the air left my lungs.

All the emotion—the fear, self-doubt, and worry—was sucked away, and my mind was left clear. Within moments I was looking at a small constellation of stars—two clustered together, one nearby, and one slightly farther away. Jonathan, the attacker, Mrs. Burns, and Addie, I placed them. But of the two close together, I wasn't sure which was who.

"Clueless woman. Getting in was the hard part. I can portal out of here in seconds," the stranger said.

I had to take a chance. I didn't know if trying to influence a mind from this state would work, or if I had to see the person. I had a fifty-

fifty chance of choosing the right light to focus on. But I didn't have time for deliberation. I chose the one farther from what I thought was Mrs. Burns.

Drop the knife! It's burning your hand! Open your hands! I threw a few commands out, hoping one would stick. I heard a scream, then a scuffle. I kept shooting commands at my target. *You can't close your hands. In fact, you can't move. Your muscles have all gone stiff.* A couple of thumps preceded a strangled cry of pain.

I opened my eyes and rushed through the hall and into the next room. Jonathan had his arms wrapped around a woman with dark hair, fair skin, and bright red lips. Mrs. Burns was standing on the blade of a knife, flattening it against the floor, and Addie was chanting again, her hands pointed at the stranger.

Footsteps thundered up the stairs and down the hall. Roman Bishop burst into the room, followed by Sheriff Kasun. The sheriff took one look around and calmly slapped handcuffs on the woman, who was standing stiff as a board. I smiled to myself.

"Where is it, witch?" Mrs. Burns cried. "Where is my pendant?"

The woman smirked at her but said nothing.

"Why don't you leave the questioning to us, Mrs. Burns?" Sheriff Kasun said. "We'll find out what she's done with it."

"Not to worry," Roman said. "It won't take us long." He flashed a truly frightening smile at the woman, who seemed to go even paler at his statement.

Having turned the woman over to the authorities, Jonathan crossed the room to put his arm around his mother, who was shaking uncontrollably—whether with rage or fear, it was hard to tell.

The sheriff and Roman filed out of the room, the woman between them, leaving me and Addie with Jonathan and his mother.

"Are you both okay?" I asked, looking them over.

Mrs. Burns took a shuddering breath. "No real harm done, dear. Thanks to you, I presume."

I felt a blush creep up my face as Jonathan looked at me in surprise. "She just dropped the knife all of a sudden. That was you?"

I nodded sheepishly. "I didn't know if I could, but I had to try. And, somehow, it worked."

Addie shook her head. "She was foolish to come in here unprotected. I guess she thought that boy would provide enough distraction to allow her to get to you, Leah."

"Well, she was right about that, I guess," Mrs. Burns said. "She was in here waiting for me when I came up. Is Helena all right? That witch was gloating about knocking her out."

"Yes, I think she'll be fine," Addie said. "I asked Elsmed to check on her, and he's probably already called Dr. Underwood."

Mrs. Burns turned to Jonathan. "Are you sure you're okay? She didn't—" She broke off, tears coming to her eyes as she realized what could have happened.

"I'm fine, Mom. Go check on Mrs. Walsh. I want to talk to Celeste for a minute."

"Okay," she said, looking at me, then back at her son. "We'll see you downstairs in a bit, then."

Addie put her arm around Mrs. Burns's shoulders as they left the room and went downstairs, leaving me alone with Jonathan.

"So . . ." I said to fill the awkward silence. It just made it seem more awkward.

"So I wanted to thank you. I don't know how you did it, but . . . thank you."

I shrugged off his gratitude.

"No, really." He put a finger under my chin and lifted my face to meet his gaze, sending a shiver through me. "I don't know what would have happened if you hadn't stepped in. My mom was going into panic mode." He sighed, dragging fingers through his longish hair. "We've had to leave our life behind so many times; all we have is each other. She can't give up the artifact, but she isn't willing to give me up for it either." He took my hand in his.

75

"What is it? The artifact, I mean."

"Mom won't tell me exactly what it does. I just know that if the wrong people get their hands on it, well . . . it could turn the tide of a war that's been going on for generations. It could mean genocide," he said, making me gasp.

"Well, you're welcome," I said quietly, unsure of what else to say.

He chuckled and leaned in, pressing a soft kiss to my cheek. "You're special, Celeste."

"So are you." I was blushing so hard now, I felt my hair was about to catch fire.

"Oh, really?" he teased.

I nodded vehemently. "Yep. It's not just anyone I rescue from wicked witches," I said with a sly grin.

He rewarded me with a deep belly laugh, then composed himself and bowed low, still holding my hand. "I am honored, my lady," he said, eliciting a giggle from me.

"So I guess you'll be out of school for a few days?"

"Yeah, at least until they find the pendant. I can't leave my mom alone while it's out there. They could send someone else to—" He broke off, and I nodded.

"Well, I know this is far from over, but in the meantime, I can bring you notes and assignments to get your mind off things while they search. Help you study?"

He hesitated, and I guessed he hadn't considered keeping up with his schoolwork, but in the end he smiled. "Sure, that would be great."

We exchanged cell numbers to keep in touch.

"Come on, we'd better go downstairs before they come looking for us," I said.

Elsmed was talking to Mr. McCabe when we reached the living room, and through the window I could see the sheriff helping the dark-haired witch into his truck, with Roman Bishop impatiently tapping the toe of his expensive-looking shoe on the sidewalk.

"You'll have to keep a close eye on him," Elsmed was saying.

"Addie will clear him of the compulsion, but he's susceptible. We don't want him caught up with this thief again."

"You have my word, Elsmed," Mr. McCabe said, giving the older man a firm handshake. "I have no intention of letting him out of my sight except to send him to school, and I'll make sure Friske has a tight leash on him as well."

"Thank you, Mike," Elsmed said. "Now let's get you back home."

As if on cue, Addie appeared from the hall to the sunroom. After nodding to Elsmed and Mr. McCabe, she proceeded to stand in front of Remy, who was still sitting in a chair, staring vacantly. She held her hands out toward him and started a low chant that went on for several minutes.

When she finished, Remy blinked rapidly and looked around with alarm, seeming as if he'd just been startled awake.

"What— Where— How—" he uttered in obvious confusion, his eyes darting from one person to the next, before landing on Mr. McCabe.

"I'll explain on the way home," Mr. McCabe said, extending an arm to rest around the boy's shoulders as he rose to his feet. "Let's leave these folks to their business." He nodded to Elsmed as he opened the front door, revealing Dr. Underwood with his hand raised to knock on it.

Once McCabe had left with Remy, Addie escorted Dr. Underwood back to the sunroom to check on Mrs. Walsh.

"Jonathan, why don't you go help your mother and Dr. Underwood," Elsmed said. "I'll see that Celeste gets home safely."

Jonathan looked to me as he nodded, touched my hand in goodbye, and disappeared down the hallway.

"Why?" I asked.

Elsmed peered down at me as he walked me home. "Would you care to expand on that?"

"Why didn't my dad, or you, or anyone tell me I was fae?"

"Well, your dad didn't—doesn't—know, and I'd like very much to keep it that way. I was . . . getting around to it."

"He doesn't know? How is that possible? My mom was fae, right?"

"Yes, and your dad is human. We have rules in this town to protect the humans from knowing too much about the supernaturals. I can't say how much your mother told him about her nature when she was alive, but after she was gone, the Court ruled that he would be better off not knowing."

"The court? What court would rule a man should be kept in the dark about his own wife—and daughter?"

"The Court of the Sun and the Moon. It's not your average civil court. It's the ruling body of this town and decides all matters of importance affecting supernatural residents and visitors. It is made up of certain members of the founding families of this town, and I am one of them."

"So we have an extra court that enforces its own rules? Is that legal?"

I could swear he rolled his eyes. "It's for the good of the town and everyone in it. What do you think would happen if someone let slip that there were supernaturals living here? Do you think we would be safe if word got out there were fae in Havenwood Falls? Or vampires? Or witches? We've learned from our past, even if the rest of the world refuses to." He fixed me with a glare that indicated that was all he was saying about that subject.

I decided to get back to the point. "How could my dad be better off not remembering my mom?"

"Oh, he remembers her. It's just that his memory is fuzzy on a few details. Humans are used to that."

"But . . . I still don't understand why."

"It's a . . . delicate issue, Celeste. Your mother's death was very . . .

unusual. Violent. It would have been traumatizing for your father to know the truth. We decided it was for the best to let him forget some of the supernatural elements, but let him retain the essence of his relationship with his wife. Trust me, it was kinder this way."

"I see," I said, my voice sounding small. "So it wasn't . . . the accident?"

The old man just shook his head.

"Will you tell me what happened to her?"

Elsmed eyed me. "Perhaps. But not tonight."

We both fell silent, our footsteps on the sidewalk reverberating through the freezing evening air.

"So what about me?"

"What about you?"

"Well, am I just left to figure things out on my own? Don't I get a faerie godmother or something to help me?"

This started in Elsmed a chuckle that soon grew into a hearty laugh, which almost seemed to threaten his breathing. "A . . . faerie . . . godmother!"

I couldn't help the smile that crept across my own face.

Once he'd caught his breath, Elsmed continued walking. "I've kept an eye on you from afar. Your abilities were mostly benign until recently, but I monitored you to make sure they didn't get out of hand. I stepped in once it became clear your awakening was beginning and you would need guidance to control your gift."

"What else can I do? I mean, is what I did in there the extent of my ability? Or is there more?"

"Each person's ability is their own. We will continue to explore the nature of yours. In addition, I would like to get you enrolled in an evening class at Sun and Moon Academy that will help you develop and hone your skills. It's a private school for supernaturals, and they specialize in helping young people master their abilities."

"*Another* class?" I whined. *First yoga, now this. I'm going to have no social life at all if he keeps signing me up for all these classes.* "I don't think

— I mean, isn't that expensive? My dad isn't exactly private-school rich."

Elsmed regarded me out of the corner of his eye. "Don't worry about tuition; just tell your father I applied for a scholarship on your behalf. I'll take care of the enrollment. You just make time in your *busy social schedule* to attend class on Thursday evenings."

"Do you listen in on everything that goes through my head?" *I sure hope not.*

Elsmed chuckled. "No, certainly not. But keeping a civil tone in your mind is good practice for maintaining one on your tongue. Respect will get you far in this town, but it must be given before it can be received."

"I'll keep that in mind," I promised.

When we arrived at my house, I was dismissed to my room while Elsmed chatted with Dad, probably about my new classes. I, for one, was exhausted, and starting to come down from the adrenaline rush of the afternoon's events.

I settled in to do homework, but found myself replaying the day in my mind. Havenwood Falls had been my home my whole life, but suddenly I felt like I didn't know anything about my own town. A town filled with supernaturals, who apparently had their own school even, and I'd been completely oblivious. What else was I blind to?

CHAPTER 9

JONATHAN

*I*t was lucky we hadn't accumulated much since we got to town, because we were moving again. Mom said she couldn't continue to put Mrs. Walsh in danger, and even though Mrs. Walsh protested, I could see the fear in her eyes. Her parents lived in the apartment above the garage; if anything happened to them because of us, my mom would never forgive herself.

Havenwood Falls wasn't the idyllic place it purported to be. I'd heard rumors in the short time I was in school that for some time now, valuable items had gone missing and more than one person had even been kidnapped. It made me wonder why my mom thought this was a safe place to come to begin with. No place was safe for us anymore. It was pretty clear to me, so I didn't know why she couldn't see that truth.

Of course, we couldn't leave town until we'd gotten the Seelie key back. My mom had finally filled me in on what exactly we'd lost. More than the simple piece of jewelry it seemed, the key would grant access to one of the most sacred places in Faerie, a source of power for the Seelie fae. If the Unseelie army infiltrated it, they could cripple the Seelie army and topple the Seelie Court. We could not let that happen.

Fortunately for them, but unfortunately for us, the key would not work on its own. It needed a password—a key to the key—to work. My mom said she didn't have the password, but she must know who did. The most important thing right now was getting that pendant back and getting on the road. If we kept moving, it would be that much harder to find us.

To be honest, though, I was getting a little tired of living constantly on the run. I felt an unexpected pang of sadness at the thought of leaving, and not for the first time, wished we could settle down somewhere for good. We hadn't been in town long enough for me to really grow attached to much, but there was one person I didn't want to say goodbye to yet: Celeste.

For now, Elsmed was moving us to one of his properties in town. There were no guarantees we'd be any safer there, but at least we wouldn't be putting anyone else in danger. I finished packing all my worldly belongings into my backpack and a single duffel bag just as my mom came into the room.

"All set?" she asked.

"Yeah, this is everything."

A sad look crossed her face. I knew this wasn't the life she imagined for me, for her family. But it was the life we got. Sometimes there were circumstances beyond your control, and you just had to roll with it. I knew it, and she knew it.

"Okay, let's go say goodbye."

My mom thanked Mrs. Walsh for her hospitality and apologized for the trouble our stay had caused her, while I waited by the door. The two women had become fast friends, and while we weren't leaving town just yet, I could see in my mom's slumped shoulders and tearing eyes that she was pulling away from the friendship in preparation for our eventual final departure.

When we finally made it out the door, Elsmed Fairchild was waiting to take us to our new temporary home.

"Good afternoon, Burns family."

"Good afternoon, Elsmed," my mother greeted him. "Thank you for giving us a place to stay until the key is found."

We loaded our meager possessions into the waiting car and piled in.

"The new house will be more secure until this all blows over," he said, as the driver pulled away from the curb. "I still think Havenwood Falls is the safest place for you both to stay, even after we've found the key and returned it to your care."

"How can you say that?" my mom blurted, earning a glare from Elsmed. She cleared her throat and ducked her head. "Respectfully, Elder, the key was stolen within weeks of our arrival here. It doesn't seem the safest place for us or it."

"By all appearances, the perpetrators of the theft are not associated with Unseelie elements. The woman who attacked you is just a money-hungry witch, and we'll get to the bottom of what brought her here. She'll forget about this place as soon as she leaves it, and won't be able to enter again. The wards on the town offer you a layer of protection you won't find anywhere else. Not to mention the residents who are able to help."

"How did she find out about the key in the first place? It's not exactly common knowledge outside fae circles."

"That's one of the questions we're trying to answer with our interrogations. Trust me, the entire Court is focused on eliminating any threats to our town's residents and visitors. It's better to be inside than out."

"I'll keep that in mind, Elsmed," Mom said, still sounding skeptical.

The car pulled up to a small Victorian house just a block from the town square. It looked well maintained, if plain, with white siding and a covered front porch. Elsmed got out and waited while we gathered our things.

"This is one of the most protected spots in town," he said, walking ahead of us toward the front door. "Addie lives only a few blocks down that way"—he pointed to one side of the house—"and your neighbor on this side, Everett Weston, is a gargoyle protector." *Wow, this town really does have one of everything.* "Across the street, of course, is the police station. Anyone would be mad to try to attack you here."

Mom looked up and down the street, anxiety still apparent on her face.

"Don't worry, Leah," Elsmed said. "We'll get all the information we need out of that witch soon enough. Roman is questioning her right now."

She pursed her lips, saying nothing.

Elsmed continued the realtor routine. "The place is furnished— two bedrooms—and there are linens in the closets, but I haven't had a chance to stock the icebox. The grocery store in Miller's Plaza should have everything you need."

"Thank you, Elsmed," my mom said. "We'll get settled in on our own. I'm sure you have a lot to do."

He nodded once and handed over the house key. "You know how to get in touch with me should you require anything else. I'll let you know when we have any news."

~

CELESTE

It was Thursday, and I was fidgety all day. Even though I knew the witch was locked up, I kept waiting for her to jump out at me from around a corner. On top of that, I would be attending my first Awakening Lab class that evening, and I'd never even been to Sun and Moon Academy before. I didn't know what to expect.

The halls of Havenwood Falls High seemed so different now that I knew they were populated by not only humans, but other supernatural species. I was still wrapping my head around the fact that I was one of them. It felt silly, but for a second I wished I had Mrs. Burns there with me to identify the kids I'd known all my life.

After school, I visited the teachers whose classes Jonathan was in but I wasn't to pick up assignments for him. As I was leaving the last one, books and folders piled high in my arms, I ran into Margaret.

"Hi, Margie."

"Celeste! There you are. Where did you go after class?"

"I'm just getting a few assignments to keep Jonathan caught up while he's out." I was also anxious to learn if they had any news on the search for the pendant, but I couldn't tell her that.

"Oh, is he okay?" Margaret said, looking concerned.

"Yeah, he just had to stay home to deal with some family stuff for a while. I'm going to go study with him now."

"Oh, I see," she said, a smile creeping onto her face. "I enjoy *studying* with Xavier, too."

I bumped her shoulder with mine, making her curls bounce. "I'm not sure if he wants to *study* like that with me."

"Of course he does," she said. "He seems like he's into you. And he wouldn't have asked you to study with him if he didn't want to spend time with you."

"Well, I kind of offered. And there was a definite hesitation before he agreed."

"Hmm, okay, well, has he made any other moves?"

"Well, he did kiss me . . ."

"*What?* Why are you—"

"On the cheek."

"Oh."

"Yeah," I said. "I felt like . . . I don't know, like his little sister or something. I mean, it was sweet, but . . ."

"But not much heat."

"Yeah."

"Well, maybe he's just shy. Give him a minute to get to know you. He won't be able to resist that charm for long."

"You think?"

She looked at me over her glasses. "I know. Now go take those books to your *study buddy*, and I'll see you tomorrow."

TRUDGING down to the town square from school was different with two loads full of books and folders. On my internship days, I'd been able to drop my things at home on the way to City Hall. By the time I got to the corner of Stuart Street and Eleventh, I was cold and wobbly on my feet, not to mention distracted by thoughts of the witch and the pendant.

Just as I was stepping onto the sidewalk from the crosswalk, my foot landed on a patch of ice. Time seemed to slow as books and papers went flying, my arms windmilling futilely for balance, and my bottom landed hard on the pavement.

"Ow."

"Are you okay?"

I looked up and into the face of arguably the hottest guy in town, Everett Weston. I mean, he was taken and probably a dozen years too old for me, but he was perfectly suitable as eye candy. I looked into his bright green eyes and tried to catch my breath.

"I-I think so," I stammered, tearing my eyes away from his to survey the damage. I was surrounded by a circle of books and papers, and my bag had fallen into the street.

Everett turned in a circle, evidently looking for a place to set down the two Coffee Haven cups in his hands, when another voice came from farther down the sidewalk.

"I've got her," Jonathan said, making my breath catch in my throat once more.

Everett and I both looked up to see him strolling down the sidewalk toward the site of my calamity, eyes fixed on mine.

"You okay with him?" Everett muttered under his breath.

I nodded. "Yeah, he's my study date," I said, a smile forming as I levered myself up to my knees so I could start gathering my things. "Thanks, Everett."

"Sure thing. Be careful," he said, then nodded to Jonathan and headed for the steps of his office and home.

Jonathan reached me and stooped to help me gather his schoolwork, then hoisted my bag onto his shoulder and held out a hand to me. I took it, the way his grip enveloped mine with warmth giving me a thrill as I pulled myself up, careful not to bump into him and knock us both to the ground again.

"Well, I almost made it," I joked.

"A valiant effort." He smiled. "Thanks for bringing all this. It's making me a little crazy sitting around waiting for something to happen."

I laughed nervously. "I know what you mean. I don't know that your Government textbook will make you any less crazy, but at least it's something to do."

We reached the door, and he held it open for me to go inside.

It was a cute space, with blue-striped furniture in the living room and a little white wooden table in the kitchen area. Mrs. Burns was on the phone in the living room, pacing back and forth nervously.

"Let's go upstairs to study," Jonathan suggested. "Mom's likely to be on the phone a while."

"Okay," I agreed, and followed him up the stairs to a sparsely decorated bedroom with a bean bag chair and a low table opposite the bed.

"Please, take the chair," he said, gesturing to the bean bag. "I imagine your behind's had enough of hard surfaces today."

I blushed, but took the offered chair. "Given my behind a lot of thought, have you?"

Now it was his turn to blush. "No more than it deserves," he said with a smile.

Someone's feeling flirty today. "So, any word on the pendant?"

He sat down on the floor beside me. "No—well, yes. They think they've got an approximate location out of the woman, but they haven't found it yet. From what I could tell, it sounded like she'd buried it in the forest somewhere. Mom's on the phone with the sheriff, and they've got a couple of wolf shifters trying to sniff out the location."

"Wolf . . . shifters," I repeated.

"Yeah, you know, they shift from human to wolf, and back."

"I see." *Wow.* My head was starting to spin again.

"Someone named Rusty, and Conall Kasun, I believe, are doing most of the tracking."

"*Deputy* Conall Kasun? Is a wolf?"

"A shifter, yes. The whole Kasun family is. They were going to ask the mountain lions for help, but they've got their hands full with making sure the boy doesn't get sucked back in."

"The boy?"

"The one that was at the house yesterday? At Mrs. Walsh's?"

"Remy. He's a . . . mountain lion?"

"Shifter."

"Uh-huh."

"You really had no idea about any of this, huh?"

I shook my head. "No."

"How is it no one ever told you? Didn't you feel . . . different?"

"Different from what? I've always felt like myself. Apparently, my mom was fae, but my dad is human. She died when I was young, and the powers that be decided it was a good idea to wipe my dad's memory, so who was there to tell me?"

"Okay, I get that. But even before your awakening, you should have had some tendencies toward your ability. Didn't anyone notice?"

"I don't think so. It's not something even I knew I was doing. I just figured I was skilled at getting people to do what I wanted. I attributed my powers of persuasion to my sweet smile and impeccable reasoning. Obviously."

He laughed at this.

"One of my first memories is of my father apologizing to my kindergarten teacher. He said I was a 'willful child,' and that he was at the end of his rope with me. Apparently, I had convinced one of the other kids in my class that he was the appointed pencil sharpener for me and my friends, and he got in trouble for spending twenty minutes at the pencil sharpener. When the teacher had the audacity to tell me I was responsible for sharpening my own pencils, I gave her the silent treatment. For the rest of the month."

"Wow. That's commitment."

"Sometime along the way, my dad and I came to an understanding, and I made my peace with school eventually, but I still don't respond well to being slighted."

"All hail Queen Celeste." He chuckled.

"Hey, I'm not so terrible," I said, pushing his shoulder. "I'm a benevolent ruler."

"Just don't get on your bad side."

"Exactly," I said with a smile.

"You're cute," Jonathan said, and touched my cheek.

"*Cute* is not a word used to describe a queen."

"Oh, of course. My apologies, Your Majesty. I meant to say, of course, delightful."

"Divine?"

He tilted his head as if considering this, then leaned closer and said, "Demure."

"Delicious."

His eyebrow quirked up at this, and his pale blue gaze held mine, only inches away now.

"How would I know if you're delicious?" he said quietly.

I shrugged. "I guess you'd have to take a taste."

Who am I right now? I was like a runaway train; the words came out of my mouth without asking my permission first.

His gaze dropped from my eyes slowly, landing on my lips, which parted at the attention.

"May I?" he asked softly, looking back into my eyes.

I nodded once.

He inched closer and gently pulled me in, his hand on my cheek moving to cradle the back of my head. I closed my eyes and felt his long lashes brush my cheek just before soft lips pressed to mine. Kissing Jonathan was like being wrapped in a warm, cozy blanket after the craziness of the last few days.

"Delectable," he said, pulling away.

"Mm" was all I could manage.

Footsteps on the stairs alerted us to company, and we sprang apart, each picking up a random book. Mrs. Burns stopped at the threshold.

"They've found it."

CHAPTER 10

JONATHAN

*C*eleste and I scrambled to our feet.

"Where was it?" I asked, relieved and worried at the same time. If the key was still out there, unguarded and uncovered, it could easily be lost or taken again.

"Buried in the forest near Mount Alexa," Mom said, her face scrunching in contempt. "I guess the witch figured no one would find it out there." She shook her head at the phone still in her hand.

"So should we go out there to meet them?" We followed my mom down the stairs.

"No," Mom said, "they're going to bring it in to the police station. Ric said we should meet him there." She finally put the phone down and headed for the coatrack by the door.

We all bundled back up in our winter jackets and headed out the door to the police station, just on the other side of the street. I held on to Celeste's hand, mostly so she wouldn't slip and fall again, but also because it felt right being connected to her. She didn't seem to object.

As we neared the door to the station, we met Elsmed Fairchild and Mathilde Augustine heading toward us from the direction of City Hall. I held open the glass door as everyone filed in, the five of us nearly filling the small waiting area just inside. While Mrs. Augustine spoke with the secretary, Elsmed pulled my mom and me aside to a corner of the room.

"We need to discuss the future plans for the safety of the key." He looked at my mom. "I think it's time to pass the mantle on."

She shook her head, her eyes going wide.

"It's all right, Leah. He's old enough."

She looked at me nervously.

My eyes darted back and forth between them. "You . . . me? You want me to guard it? Why not Mom?"

Elsmed put a hand on my shoulder. "You're of age now, son. And it seems too many people know of your mother's guardianship. Time to pass the torch, and perhaps you can stop running for a while."

I laughed out loud at this, causing Celeste to turn her head toward us from where she stood next to Mrs. Augustine.

"Stop running?" I said to Elsmed. "We haven't stopped running my whole life." I glanced at my mom and saw her cast her gaze to the floor. "Now that we've lost the key once, we've got to run even farther and faster than before."

"Slow down, Jonathan," Elsmed said. "I heard your mother yesterday, and we've been working on a plan to throw any pursuers off your scent. The unique thing about Havenwood Falls is that anyone who comes here and leaves again won't remember this place, or what occurred while they were here. We can send out a false key with the witch. She'll think she's got the real thing, and once she leaves our borders, she won't have any recollection of you or how she got it."

"Won't they come looking for us again? What's to stop the process from repeating?"

"We'll send her on a wild goose chase for the password. It will keep her busy for some time and give us a chance to make progress on finding out who her employer is, since she's lied about that. By the time they discover the key's a fake, we'll have put an end to all this trouble."

"And if you don't?"

"If we don't, you're still in the most protected place in the earth realm. No worse off than you were when you arrived here."

Mom looked at me with worry in her deep blue eyes. "Are you ready for this responsibility?" she asked.

I nodded, amazed that she was even considering this plan. I was ready, though. Happy, even, to take this burden from my mother, to take on the duty that my father carried before me. Before he died, he had explained to me that the burden of protecting the pendant would fall to me someday. "I am."

Elsmed nodded. "We can disguise the real key so that it is unrecognizable to anyone who saw it before. Mathilde is skilled in such magic, and it will be further hidden by your glamour, Jonathan."

"All right," I said, putting an arm around my mother, who was still shaking with nervous energy.

We looked up as the sheriff came into the police station, a small iron box in his hand. A slight wave of nausea swept through me. Being close to iron had that effect on me, and I could tell the other fae were feeling the signature weakness as well, though less than we would have felt outside the protection Havenwood Falls afforded us. The sheriff told the secretary he needed "the big room," and tilted his head to indicate we should follow him. We did, along with Mrs. Augustine and Celeste.

We all entered a space that looked much like a conference room, with a large table and several chairs. Sheriff Kasun closed the door behind us and invited everyone to take a seat.

"Well, it took us a little while, but we found it. Is this the item that was stolen from you?" He opened the box to reveal my mom's pendant inside, nestled on a velvet cushion.

Mom broke out in tears, nodding her head and reaching for the pendant.

"Yes, that's it," I responded, because she was clearly unable to get words out at the moment.

Mom lifted the gold pendant to her chest, clutching it so tightly in her fist I thought she might crush the thing.

"Thank you, Ric," Elsmed said. "The box should be processed for evidence right away. It did not belong to Mrs. Burns, but might hold a clue to identifying whoever really hired the witch."

"Sure, I'll hold on to it. Why don't you all keep the room a few minutes, until you're ready to leave," he said, looking at my mom, who was still racked with sobs.

"And please call Wieland Manos and have him meet us here right away."

"Okay," Ric said, clearly not understanding the purpose behind the command, but not about to question Elsmed Fairchild.

"Give our appreciation to Rusty and Conall, please, Ric," Mrs. Augustine said as he opened the door.

He nodded his acknowledgment and left, closing the door behind him. Elsmed and Mathilde quickly put their heads together and started discussing something I supposed we weren't meant to hear.

I leaned over to Celeste, who had taken the seat on the other side of my mother, and whispered, "Manos?"

She turned her head and whispered in my ear, "Jeweler."

Aha.

We waited for Manos, my mom slowly recovering from her crying bout and releasing her vise grip on the pendant. Celeste laid a comforting hand on Mom's shoulder.

About ten minutes later, the sheriff escorted a man into the room. Wieland Manos was medium height, with green eyes and blond, almost white, hair. He smiled as he entered, though it was obvious he had no idea why he'd been summoned.

"Wieland, thank you for coming," Elsmed said, rising to shake hands with the man. "I don't know if you've had the pleasure of meeting Leah Burns and her son, Jonathan?" He waved a hand in our direction.

"Ah, no. It's nice to make your acquaintance," he said.

I rose to shake his hand, and my mother managed a smile.

"Please, sit," Elsmed said, taking his own seat again. "We have need of your services—and your discretion," he continued, sharpening his gaze at Manos to make his point. "You are skilled with gold filigree, are you not?"

Manos puffed out his chest a bit. "Yes, it is a specialty of mine," he answered.

"Excellent. We need you to replicate this piece exactly," Elsmed said, gesturing to my mother to show the pendant.

She reluctantly opened her hand and laid it on the table, its surface shimmering in the fluorescent lights.

"Oh, that is exquisite," Manos said, reaching out to pick up the piece of jewelry. My mom gasped and reached out as if to take it back, but Celeste held her hand and put an arm around her shoulders to calm her.

Manos took a jeweler's loupe out of his pocket and examined the necklace closely, turning it over in his hand. "Do you want a chain like this too?"

"Yes, exactly the same."

Manos bent his head to study the chain again, then nodded. "I can do it. No problem. I'll have it ready in two days' time."

"That will have to do," Elsmed said. "I'm afraid we cannot let it out of Mrs. Burns's possession, though. Can you craft it from memory?"

Mr. Manos looked less sure of this proposition. "Can I take some pictures?" he said.

Elsmed considered this, exchanging glances with Mathilde before answering.

"Yes, you may photograph the piece, but all images must be destroyed once the piece is finished. No copies, Wieland, digital or otherwise. Understood?"

"Yes, sir. No problem."

We all waited and watched in silence as Manos took out his phone and photographed the necklace, turning it this way and that to capture every detail. I felt myself growing wistful. After seeing the necklace on my mother every single day of my life, I would miss seeing its delicate form.

Once Manos was finished, he stood to go. "I'll give you a call when it's ready," he said.

"Thank you, Wieland," Elsmed said, standing to shake hands again and close the door behind the jeweler.

"Now there's one thing left to do," Elsmed said, turning to Mrs. Augustine.

"May I?" Mrs. Augustine asked my mother, who gave her a nod and looked sorrowfully at her pendant.

Mrs. Augustine picked up the key and closed her hands around it, holding them close in front of her and bowing her head. She looked like she was praying, eyes closed and speaking words too softly for us to hear. After a minute, she looked up at me.

"Do you want a magical tracker on it?" she asked.

I looked to my mom, who gave me a slight nod of acceptance. We both knew this could be dangerous if the tracker was compromised, but could save us if anything like what had happened over the last few days were to transpire again.

"Yes, please," I told Mrs. Augustine.

"Come here," she said.

She bowed her head and mumbled some more words over the key as I came over to stand beside her, then stood herself and placed her still-folded hands against my chest. Now that I was standing close to her, I could hear the words she said, but couldn't make sense of them. Suddenly, she stopped speaking and looked up, opening her hands.

As I looked down into her open hands, I saw a completely different piece of jewelry. It was a tarnished silver disc with a Celtic knot design embossed on it, strung onto what looked like a leather cord. And I could feel it. It was not uncomfortable, but it felt like a string had been pulled taut between my heart and the pendant, and I knew I could find it with my eyes closed.

"The feeling will go away once you put it on, and return if you take it off," she said.

"He won't take it off," Mom said.

"No, you won't need to," said Mrs. Augustine. "The cord looks like leather, but it's not. It's stronger than steel and resistant to water. And the disc won't polish if you rub it, so don't bother trying." She smiled.

"It's perfect," I said, lifting it over my head to rest around my neck. "Thank you, Mrs. Augustine."

"My pleasure, dear," she said, backing away and brushing imaginary dust from her skirt.

I looked to my mom, whose eyes were tearing up again. I rounded the table again to stand beside her. "Don't worry, Mom. Nothing is changing, except I'm wearing it now. Everything stays the same."

"Oh, honey," she said. "Nothing's the same. I knew this day would come, but I didn't imagine it would be so soon. We will be okay, though. We will be okay." She sounded as if she was trying to reassure herself.

Elsmed cleared his throat, drawing everyone's attention to him once again. "All right, we've done all we need to for now. Ric will keep the witch locked up until the necklace is ready, and then we'll drop her off well outside the border and let her lead us to this person she called the Collector. Then we can find out what brought her here, and prevent it from happening again."

"I'll walk back with you to get my stuff," Celeste said. We all made our way out of the police station.

"Don't forget your class tonight, Celeste," Elsmed warned as we parted ways. "You're already registered, and I've asked Gianna's mother to give you a ride home from class."

Celeste blanched. "Gianna's . . ."

"A witch, of course, like me," Mrs. Augustine finished for her.

I saw the light dawn on Celeste as she put it together. "O-of course," she managed to get out. "That sounds great, thanks."

We turned to go our separate ways.

"I don't know that I'll ever get used to finding out that people I've known all my life are not . . . people."

"Oh, we're all people, dear," Mom said. "Just different kinds."

"I guess so," Celeste mused, still looking a bit dazed.

"What class are you taking?" I asked to try to snap her out of it.

"It's called Awakening Lab. It's for practice, I guess, to learn control of your abilities. I thought it was just for fae, but I guess not."

"You know what they say, dear," my mom said.

"What's that?" Celeste asked.

"It takes all kinds to make a world."

∾

CELESTE

THE WALK to Sun and Moon Academy was just as far from the Burnses' place as Havenwood Falls High, and I was worn out from a long day when I arrived at the Academy. Somehow, even though I'd lived in Havenwood Falls my whole life, I'd never been on the Academy's campus. It was beautiful, even though I couldn't see much of the grounds because by the time I arrived, full dark was descending.

I passed through a stone arch into a courtyard surrounded by stately buildings. It felt almost as if I'd wandered onto a college campus, though there were few people around at this time of the evening. I followed signs to the Falls Campus, where my class was being held, and found myself trailing behind a few other students headed the same way.

Luckily, they knew where to go, so I didn't waste time searching for the classroom. I should have been dead on my feet after the day I'd had, but somehow I felt more energized the farther I ventured onto the campus. My footsteps echoed in the courtyards. The nearby waterfall was mostly iced over from the winter's cold, and only a slight trickle could be heard.

As I took a seat, I again found myself wondering what species were in the room. To my surprise, Gianna's mom—Ronya Augustine, Mathilde's daughter-in-law—entered the class a moment later and introduced herself as the instructor. My jaw almost dropped to the floor. I supposed I should just get used to being astonished.

After a few preliminary announcements and ground rules (no active practicing on your classmates unless specifically requested to do so by the teacher), we were split into small groups—shift control, harnessing energy, appetite management, mental exercise, and physical exercise. I went up to Ms. Augustine after the assignments, while the other students rearranged themselves into groups.

"Excuse me, Ms. Augustine?"

"Welcome to class, Celeste. I'm so excited to get to work with you," she said.

"Me too. But I think I was assigned to the wrong group."

"Oh, let me see." She looked at her list. "No, I have you in appetite management."

"Shouldn't I be in mental exercise, though? I mean, I don't have an appetite problem"—I looked at my group and gulped—"not like other students might."

"No, of course," Ms. Augustine said. "Every student here is unique. We rotate you through groups as you gain proficiency in the study areas, but we have to take things in order or there could be repercussions. Right now, the first priority for you is appetite management."

I shook my head, still not understanding, but let her shoo me back to my group. She gave us an assignment to take a few minutes to identify our most pressing desires before we started to brainstorm ways to manage them. The other members of my group introduced themselves. Otis was a tall boy with longish dark hair and brown eyes. I had seen him around Havenwood Falls High, but didn't have any classes with him. Delia was a petite blonde with green eyes whom I'd not met before. We pulled our desks into a circle to talk.

"Blood," said Delia, conspicuously looking everywhere but at me. "Always blood." *I guess she didn't need a few minutes for that one,* I thought to myself, and made a mental note to keep my distance from her.

"The hunt," said Otis. "I dream about hunting, and now I'm even starting to daydream about it. It's distracting me from school, friends, everything."

They looked at me. *My turn.* What could I say? I didn't have any uncontrollable urges that I knew about. I had become aware of certain strong feelings about Jonathan, but I wasn't about to share them with these practical strangers, and certainly not in front of Ms. Augustine.

"I-I don't know," I said.

"Think about it," Ms. Augustine said, walking up to our group from behind me. "If not for yourself, what do you most want for someone else, right now?"

Other than to be not here? I closed my eyes to shut out the looks Delia was giving me. I was suddenly feeling a little unsafe. *Like poor Mrs. Burns. How awful it must have been to be violated that way, to be attacked not once, but twice.* I started getting angrier the more I thought about it. *How dare that witch prey on innocent people like that! And for what, a little money? She just attacked Mrs. Walsh in her own home!* The events of the past couple of days were finally catching up to me, and I was so enraged I forgot what question I was even supposed to be answering.

"What is it you want, Celeste?" Ms. Augustine said quietly.

"Revenge," I blurted out, surprising myself, and judging by their expressions, those around me.

"Whoa," said the hunter.

"Dark," said the bloodthirsty girl.

I looked at Ms. Augustine. "Good work," she said. "Now brainstorm ideas for managing your desires." She looked at each of us with a smile and turned to go speak to another group.

"Do you drink animal blood?" Otis asked Delia.

"Yes," she said, "but it's not exactly . . . satisfying. I'm trying to get off the human blood bank supply. I don't like the idea of feeding off my friends and neighbors, you know?"

"Yeah, totally," I said. *Wow, maybe this girl isn't so bad after all.*

"How about you?" she said to Otis. "Don't you get to hunt with your family?"

"Yeah," he said, "when the weather's nice. But my mom won't let me go out in the cold. She says she's afraid of finding a pup popsicle in the morning."

"Have you talked to the coach at school?" I asked. "Maybe some other kind of physical activity could help out."

"No, but you're right, I should. There are a lot of shifters on the football team. I bet he has some sort of regimen worked out with them."

Huh. I guess that makes sense.

"So what about you?" Otis said.

"Me, well," I said, "I've started yoga. I've heard meditation helps with . . . I guess, keeping my cool. I just get so *angry* sometimes at the injustices I see."

"My dad always says, 'Empathy is the best prevention for anger.' Maybe that's something to work on?" Otis suggested.

"I *do* have empathy, though," I rebutted. "I have empathy for the victims, the ones who deserve it."

"Everyone is a victim of their own circumstance," Ms. Augustine said, circling back to us. "And everyone is deserving of empathy. Once you accept that, you may find you are better able to use your ability for positive purposes. It is not a tool for punishment but for empowerment."

"Empowerment," I parroted, turning the idea over in my head.

"Yes. Think about whom you could lift up with your ability, and you'll be surprised, I think, at the positive impact you can make."

CHAPTER 11

CELESTE

*S*chool on Friday felt like an eternity. I was hopping with nervous energy, and couldn't stand the thought of another attack. There was no chance of me focusing on what my teachers were actually saying. At least it gave me plenty of time to think on what Mrs. Augustine had said the evening before. There had to be a way I could use my anger and turn it to a positive purpose.

In English Lit, I resolved to do something to help get rid of the witch once and for all. Even with the return of the key, the threat to Jonathan and his mom still lingered. I just didn't trust that the witch would go straight to the mastermind of the theft if she was driven outside of town and dropped off by the authorities. Something told me she was a little smarter than that. She needed an extra push.

In Bio, I began to hatch a plan that would either be an amazing win or a spectacular failure. If I could use my ability to make her think she was getting away clean, we might have a better chance at tracking down the person who was really behind the theft, and maybe prevent it from happening again. Maybe it would even convince Jonathan's mom that they could stay in Havenwood Falls and stop living on the run. By the final bell, I couldn't wait to get out of school, and practically ran to City Hall to meet Elsmed and run my plan by him.

"Absolutely not," Elsmed said when I explained my idea to him.

"But—" I started.

"What makes you think we need your help tracking this witch, Celeste?" Elsmed thundered. "We've been protecting this town for many more decades than you've been alive, and I think we know what we're doing by now." His stare had turned angry, and my excitement shriveled up and turned to a sour ball in my stomach.

"I just . . . I thought . . . maybe I could help, and then the Burnses wouldn't have to worry about another . . . ." I trailed off, realizing I probably sounded idiotic to him. A teenage girl helping the supernatural protectors of the town? It even sounded ridiculous to me, once I really thought about it.

Elsmed's expression softened slightly. "And how do you think you can help, exactly? We have expert trackers ready to follow her to whoever is behind this. What do you think you can add to our efforts?" His voice took on a tone of condescension, as if he were speaking to a child. I supposed, to him, that was exactly how it felt.

"Well, what if she opens a portal when you let her loose? How will you track her then?"

"The same way we'll track her if she opens a portal from Havenwood Falls. Our witches can detect the approximate location of the portal's destination if they are there when it's opened. How is your way any better?"

"Because I can control where she intends to go with her portal. She found her way into Havenwood Falls, so she's smarter than the average hunter. Who's to say she won't portal to another location first to put us off her trail?"

"Why would she? She won't remember anything about the town once she passes the border. She wouldn't recognize Sheriff Kasun if he were standing right next to her, once she's outside the boundary."

"Well, she clearly had a plan to find Havenwood Falls before she got here. There's no reason to think she doesn't have one for getting out—one that takes the memory spell into consideration."

Elsmed gave me a long look. "Why shouldn't we have one of our witches compel her to give up the location of her employer?"

"So you haven't already had them questioning her about that? Using compulsion and any other techniques at their disposal? It took a day of interrogation just to get her to give up that it was in the woods somewhere, and it took the shifters' tracking to do the rest. She must have some protection against compulsion. But she's already given up her protection against my ability."

The look on his face told me I had hit a nerve. He glanced to where the black stone on a cord Remy had worn still sat on his desk, undoubtedly protected by some spell or another. "I'll take your comments under advisement," he said, "and discuss the matter with the Court."

I nodded, knowing enough to hold my tongue after that small victory.

For the remainder of the afternoon, he helped me practice quickly reaching a meditative state, locating other minds in proximity, and even let me push a few harmless thoughts into people's minds. It was hilarious seeing the maintenance man at Elsmed's door, completely confused by his unexplained appearance there.

We learned that while I could sometimes maintain my concentration through Elsmed's speaking directly into my mind, often it broke my focus, so we stuck to audible communication for the most part.

The next day, though, I heard Elsmed's voice in my mind. Unfortunately, I was "studying" with Jonathan at the time. I had to excuse myself to have a mental chat with my mentor about what the Court decided. He didn't give me any details about their deliberations, of course, but said they agreed that the witch seemed to have protections against their interrogations thus far, and that they had nothing to lose by trying my idea.

Tomorrow, he told me, they would arrange for me to be there when they transported the witch out of town for banishment, in human handcuffs so she could escape without suspecting they were letting her loose when I pushed her in the direction they wanted. Addie would be there to trace the portal to its destination. If my influence didn't work, there was a chance the witch would escape without anyone being able to track her. But if it did, they might gain a clue to whom the witch worked for and how they came to target the Seelie key.

The pressure of keeping the artifact—and the Burnses—safe didn't descend on me until I tried to sleep that night. Then, my mind raced through all the possibilities of how the plan could go wrong. My heart started racing and my stomach was in knots. I didn't sleep a wink.

On Sunday, I met Elsmed at City Hall, and we walked over to the police station together. I was still nervous as hell, but a little comforted to know that at least Jonathan and his mom were safe at home, and wouldn't be bothered by the criminal witch again.

"Everything ready?" Elsmed said by way of greeting Sheriff Kasun when we entered the station.

"Yes, sir," the sheriff replied. "She's cuffed for transport with the regular human cuffs, and I've got the box already processed for evidence and ready to go. You have the necklace?"

"Here it is," Elsmed said, pulling out of his pocket a gold chain with a pendant that looked exactly like the one Mrs. Burns had worn.

Sheriff Kasun took the piece of jewelry from Elsmed, examining it. "Manos does good work," he said, shaking his head. "I'd never be able to tell the difference by looking at it."

"Let's hope it fools the witch and her employer," Elsmed replied.

The sheriff nodded and placed the necklace in the box, closing it again.

"Where is Addie? She was supposed to meet us here," Elsmed said, though it sounded less like a question and more like a complaint.

"Sorry I'm late," Addie's voice preceded her through the front door.

"Good of you to join us," Elsmed said, giving her some serious side-eye.

Addie glanced at me with a reassuring smile. It was only then I realized I'd been wringing my hands and probably looked every bit the nervous wreck I was. I took a deep breath to calm myself and then kept at it when it didn't do a damn thing.

"Do you need to do any preparation before we set her loose?" the sheriff asked.

"I need a minute," I said, looking for a decent place to focus, when a thought occurred to me. "Won't she recognize me?" I asked. "She saw me at the house the other day."

"Sit down and face toward the wall," Elsmed said. "I'll block her view of you."

I did as he said, taking deep breaths and forcing my pulse into a slow, steady rhythm, which I used to put myself into a meditative state. Against the darkness of my eyelids, three lights hovered nearby, while a few others glowed somewhat farther away.

"Ready," I intoned.

"Addie, need anything?" the sheriff asked.

"No, I'm good. Anything I did would tip her off, anyway. I can read portals without any prep."

Addie went to a spot around an interior wall, where she would be able to see the portal, but the witch wouldn't see her.

"All right, showtime," the sheriff said, leaving the box on the counter and going through a heavy door, where I guessed the jail cells were.

"Focus," Elsmed said quietly. "They're coming."

I concentrated on the lights moving around in the station. There were a few that remained relatively stationary, but I saw the sheriff and the witch moving together toward the door he'd disappeared through a moment before. I heard the door open, then Elsmed muttered under his breath, "She's in front."

I focused on the light that was jerking back and forth, probably trying to free herself from her restraints.

"We found your little treasure, and we're returning it to its rightful owner," Sheriff Kasun said. "The Court has ruled that your punishment for your misdeeds is banishment, though if you ask me, it should have been much harsher."

The woman cackled, just like I'd imagined a witch would when I heard fairy tales about them as a kid. "You can't keep me out," she said. "I can come back here anytime I like."

"We can, and we will. There's nothing here for you anymore, anyway," Elsmed broke in. "The poor family you attacked fled as soon as you were captured, and where they've gone, your kind can't follow."

"Is that so?" she said. "I'm sure the Collector will pay handsomely for that information. Thank you." I thought I could hear Elsmed rolling his eyes.

"Cuffs!" Sheriff Kasun called, and I prepared myself to strike.

"Now," I heard Elsmed whisper, and I sent the first message to the witch.

"*Take the box with the key,*" I shoved into her mind. "*Steal the iron box, the one where you hid the key.*" The scrape of the box being swiped off the counter reached my ears.

Suddenly, my lungs filled with fire and my concentration fell apart. Coughs racked my chest. I struggled to breathe, wondering what the hell was going on.

The witch's laugh rang in my ears. Clearly, she was unaffected. What had she used? Pepper spray? A spell to make the air unbreathable? Whatever it was, it was working. I looked up at Elsmed and panicked when I saw him coughing too.

"You think you can confine me with ordinary handcuffs and concrete walls?" the witch asked no one in particular. "It's a wonder you all have lasted this long. You lot are clueless. Or maybe just powerless."

Crouching low as if to get under the cloud of invisible smoke, I saw Addie, seemingly unaffected, pulling items from her pockets, her lips moving nonstop. I couldn't hear what she was saying, but it must have been some powerful magic, because the witch appeared to be rooted in place, and after what seemed like several long minutes, but must have been only seconds, the air began to clear.

"Brought your own witch, did you, fools?" she screeched. "No matter. I have more spells at my disposal than she's ever heard of."

In between gasping breaths, I peeked over the police station's front counter and saw the witch pulling beads off her necklace. In her hands, they twisted and flattened, turning into gleaming throwing stars before my eyes. I ducked as she started flinging them around the room, while Addie started frantically waving her hands, presumably doing something to prevent the weapons from meeting their targets.

Holy crap. This woman was a walking arsenal. We needed to get ahead of this quickly. Addie was holding her off, but if she missed any one of those stars, we could have a serious problem. I needed to get my head together and finish what we started.

Fear rose up in my throat and threatened to choke me again. I sat cross-legged, closed my eyes, and imagined myself pushing that fear back down with both hands. *Now is not the time for doubt,* I told myself firmly. *Jonathan needs you to put an end to this.* With that thought lodged in my brain, I took four deep breaths—ignoring the blades whirring above my head—and saw the lights corresponding to each mind in the room.

"Focus on the one in the center," Elsmed said. "We've got her surrounded."

I found her light, and everything else fell away. "*Make a portal to the last place you saw the one who sent you after the pendant,*" I pushed at the witch, with every ounce of willpower in me.

There was a pause in the assault. I no longer heard the *thunk* of metal lodging in walls or the *whoosh* of near misses. After a moment of silence, I repeated the command, pleading with the universe to make this plan work. Nothing.

"Make a portal to the one who sent you after the pendant." I pushed it at her over and over, repeating it like a mantra, until I heard a strange ripping sound, and I knew she had done it.

"Your feeble spells have no hold on me," the woman gloated. "Better luck next time!"

There was a shuffling of footsteps, followed by the sound of one person running, and then the ripping sound again. The witch's light disappeared from my vision. I opened my eyes and rose to look around, not believing she was actually gone.

"Got it," Addie exclaimed.

"Was that—" Sheriff Kasun began.

"It was indeed," Elsmed cut him off. "I will inform the Court of this development. We will convene soon to discuss next steps."

The sheriff nodded and went about folding up his cuffs and tucking them away, as if we hadn't just released a money-crazed evil witch into the world.

"She won't remember this place to come back here, Celeste," Elsmed said. "And if by chance she does, the wards have already been set to cast her out and alarm us immediately. There's nothing more to worry about."

"But . . . the person behind this? Did you see where they were?"

Elsmed looked at Sheriff Kasun. "We got a solid lead, and the professionals will follow up on it. It definitely wasn't fae, Unseelie or otherwise. Your part in this is over, and very much appreciated. Thank you, my dear."

I let out the breath I hadn't realized I had been holding. It worked, and I didn't screw up and put the Burnses or the whole town in danger.

"You're welcome," I said. "I'm glad I could help."

"If you could do me one more favor?"

"Sure," I said.

"Would you inform the Burnses that the attacker is safely out of Havenwood Falls, and they are out of danger? I'll expect to hear from them about their permanent residency status by the end of the week."

"I'll let them know."

"Good girl. Run along now. I've got important business to attend to."

~

JONATHAN

SOMEONE WAS EITHER USING a jackhammer on the front door or urgently wanted to see us. I ran to the door to see which it was and saw Celeste standing there, her cheeks flushed as if she'd been running.

"Hey," I said.

"Hey, can I come in?" she said, out of breath.

"Sure." I stepped aside so she could fly by me in a flurry of excitement.

"What's going on?" Mom asked from the kitchen as I closed the door and helped Celeste out of her coat.

"It's done," Celeste exclaimed, a smile splitting her face. "The wicked witch is gone. Our plan worked."

"Plan?"

"Yeah, Elsmed's and mine. I made her open a portal to the location of whoever sent her here, so the authorities could make sure they don't send someone else."

"Oh, and where is that?"

"Well, I don't know. I had my eyes closed."

Mom's face fell.

"But don't worry! Addie and Elsmed and the sheriff saw, and they're working on pursuing it. They said it definitely wasn't Unseelie. But the important part is, she's gone."

"And the necklace?" I asked.

"Yep, she took the fake with her."

"Oh. Well, good," Mom said. She looked like she couldn't decide whether to be relieved or worried.

"It's all going to be fine," Celeste reassured us, nearly tripping over her own words. "Elsmed said the wards are set to make sure she can't come back, and if she even tries, it will send up an alarm."

"Sounds good," I said. "And thank you."

"I'm so happy I was able to do it. I was nervous I wouldn't get the timing right, and she would get away, but I did it. And it worked! Wow."

I laughed. She was clearly excited about using her ability, and her energy was infectious. I pulled her in for a hug.

"Oh, there's one more thing," Celeste said, her words slowing and her face dropping.

"What's that, dear?" Mom said.

Her whole demeanor changed, and she glanced down, as if she couldn't look us in the eyes while she delivered this next message.

Shit, this must be bad.

"Elsmed said he wants to hear from you by the end of the week about whether you'll remain in town as permanent residents."

"Oh," Mom said.

Celeste looked up at her now, worry crossing her face.

"I know it's not my decision to make, Mrs. Burns, but I really do hope you decide to stay. It's such a nice place to live, and usually very safe. And, well, I haven't known you for very long, but—" She blushed. "I just don't want you to leave."

My mom smiled for the first time since Celeste had walked through the door. "We like you too, Celeste. We will discuss it, and we'll let Elsmed know. Thank you for your bravery today, and for being such a good friend to us. It must be a very special place to have people like you in it."

Celeste rushed to my mom and enveloped her in a hug. "You are very special to me, too," she said. "Who knows how long it would have taken Elsmed to tell me the truth if you hadn't spilled the beans?" She laughed.

My mom laughed with her and invited her to stay for dinner, but Celeste wanted to get home to her father.

"I'm afraid he's been working too hard. I haven't been around much these past couple of weeks, and someone's got to make sure he's eating and sleeping and stuff," she said with a smile. I got the sense she was only half joking.

"Okay, go ahead home. Jonathan will keep you updated."

I walked her to the door and gave her another hug as I helped her put her coat back on.

"Talk soon," I whispered in her ear, and gave her a quick peck on the cheek.

She winked at me and disappeared into the frigid afternoon.

CHAPTER 12

CELESTE

TWO MONTHS LATER

"*M*argaret! Finally," I said, opening the front door to find her there, looking perfect, her curly hair in a complicated twist and her new glasses daintily perched on her nose.

"That's what you're wearing?" she said.

I didn't think it was *that* bad.

"No, no, no. Come on, we still have time," she continued, marching up the stairs, dragging me along behind her.

"What's wrong with this one, exactly?" I looked down at my blue A-line dress made of raw silk and studded with silvery beads. I thought it was lovely.

"What are you, a nun? That one says, 'Admire me from a distance, but don't touch.'"

"Well, yes, that's what my father wanted it to say."

"Where's that black dress we found last week at Callie's?"

"The one with the plunging neckline—I mean waistline? It's behind the closet door," I admitted.

"Yes! That one is hot. The gossamer sleeves are so perfect. And the slit up the side? Epic."

"But my dad is downstairs, and he insists on pictures," I reminded her.

"Okay, okay," she said. "We can do this. We are two intelligent, resourceful ladies, and we are kicking this prom's ass." She bustled around my room, opening drawers and cabinets until she found what she was looking for. "Aha!" she exclaimed.

"My underwear drawer is not going to help with this problem, Margie," I said, rolling my eyes.

"But this will," she said, lifting a black camisole from the drawer. "Put it on under the dress now and lose it when we get to the dance."

"Oh wow, I forgot I had that. Great idea. I'm so glad winter is over," I sighed, "but the coats did make it easier to dress."

"Okay, change quick. Xavier will be here soon."

I changed out of the lovely pale blue and into the racy, flowy, swirly floor-length black silk.

"Hand me those strappy shoes, would you?" I asked.

She helped me put the shoes on and touch up my makeup, then we were both tromping down the stairs, her in frothy pink, and me in fluttery black.

"How do we look, Dad?" I said, clutching Margaret's hand.

"Stunning, of course. But what happened to the other dress?"

"It just wasn't right for prom, Dad. I'll wear it another time, I promise."

"Okay, well you are lovely either way. Let me take some pictures before you go."

We posed for my dad and then a knock on the door announced our ride. My dad answered the door, and Xavier came in, greeting Margaret with a hug and a kiss on the cheek. Behind him, in a tuxedo that made him look scorching hot, was Jonathan.

"Come in, come in," my dad said. "I need pictures before you head out."

We all crowded together and grinned for more photos.

"Now you take care of these girls, and treat them like the princesses they are," my dad said.

"Yes, sir," the boys said in unison. Jonathan caught my eye and winked, his blue eyes twinkling in the light.

I couldn't help the grin that crept across my face and stayed the rest of the night, fixed there by the boy who couldn't hide his heart from my will.

We hope you enjoyed this story in the Havenwood Falls High series of novellas featuring a variety of supernatural creatures. If you liked *Willful*, we think you might enjoy these HFH books as well (read on for an excerpt of *Cast in Moonlight*):

Awaken the Soul by Michele G. Miller
Fata Morgana by E.J. Fechenda
Reclamation by AnnaLisa Grant
Cast in Moonlight by Ali Winters

ABOUT THE AUTHOR

Liz Ferry writes stories so they stop bouncing around the inside of her head and keeping her up at night. This novella is her debut long-form fiction work, but she plans to write more. When she's not writing, Liz typically occupies herself with reading and editing other authors' books. She lives in sunny Miami, Florida, with her husband, two boys, and a herd of cats.

ACKNOWLEDGMENTS

Writing this book has been an incredible experience. First thanks go to my husband, Scott, for supporting me in everything I do, and my parents, for being perennial cheerleaders. Special thanks go to my boys for being my inspiration and constant source of new ideas.

Many thanks to Kristie Cook, who came up with this amazing plan to get a bunch of talented authors together to create something fantastic. I'm so happy to be involved in this ambitious project. Thanks also to Kristie and SF Benson for polishing this story with their editorial eyes.

To all the Havenwood Falls authors, it has been an absolute delight to work with each and every one of you. I have been so impressed with the collaboration and joint world-building in our little group, as well as the kick-ass stories you all have written.

Thanks to E.J. Fechenda, Morgan Wylie, Susan Burdorf, T.V. Hahn, Kristen Yard, Belinda Boring, R.K. Ryals, Nadirah Foxx, Victoria Escobar, Victoria Flynn, Amy Hale, and Kristie Cook for allowing me to use your characters.

Special thanks to Randi Cooley Wilson, not only for use of her characters Everett, Graysin, and Roman, and not only for giving me the push I needed to pitch this story, and then again to keep at it when I got bogged down, but also for introducing me to the Havenwood Falls project, taking a chance on me as an editor, and being an awesome client who made me realize work could be fun.

Finally, thank you, dear reader, for taking a chance on me as an author, for joining us on this journey, and for loving our characters and stories as much as we do.

AN EXCERPT

Cast in Moonlight (A Havenwood Falls High Novella) Ali Winters

More than anything, Clarke Price hates the cold, so when she and her mom pick up in the middle of winter to move to the small town of Havenwood Falls in the Rocky Mountains, she is less than thrilled. On the way to their new home, their car hits a patch of black ice, sending them into a ditch. When Clarke wakes up, she finds herself stuck with an aunt she's never met, while her mom recovers in the hospital. She's never felt so alone.

While Clarke grapples with impossible truths about the town, her family, and the unbelievable realization that she's a witch, she keeps running into a stunning guy with gorgeous eyes who turns her into her least favorite cliché. He's rude, always around, and has a knack for bringing out her argumentative side. But even that isn't enough to dampen her growing attraction to him.

But can Clarke trust this handsome stranger, or is he responsible for the accidents that have nearly taken her life—twice? And what about the nightmares that feel like a dire warning that something bad is coming?

More than just her life rests on Clarke finding the truth in time.

CAST IN MOONLIGHT

BY ALI WINTERS

I crack open my eyes and instantly regret it. Bright florescent lights flicker above, accompanied by the harsh glare of sunlight through the window, and an annoying, constant beep. I squeeze my eyes shut before I can focus on anything and groan, trying to roll over. I can't. It hurts too much. Every inch of my body aches, and I think every part of me must be bruised.

Voices murmur nearby. I can't make out what they're saying. One belongs to a man, the other to a woman. I don't know who they are. The talking stops as I reach up to place a hand over my splitting head.

There's a tug on my hand, and I realize I'm attached to something. *What happened? Where am I?*

I force my eyes open again. White walls, a soft blue knitted blanket draped over my legs, and a railing on either side of my bed. I'm in the hospital, or at least something like one. The room is small. There's not really much to it.

Before I can fully get my bearings, a woman approaches. The one who must have been talking to the man in a white coat just outside the door.

"Oh good, Clarke, you're awake," she says.

It takes me a moment, but I recognize her from pictures Mom showed me years ago. The two of them on a road trip in the nineties, the summer before college, taking selfies before it was even a thing.

Looking at her face is like looking into a mirror where I've aged, though only slightly, perhaps only by a few years. But unlike me, she has a sense of style. I swear she has hardly changed since those pictures were taken. She's slender, with brown hair just past her shoulders. Where hers is wavy, mine is straight, but her brown eyes match mine perfectly. I know she's family. Considering I've only heard stories about one distant relative, there's no one else she could be.

"Aunt Michelle?" I manage to croak out. My throat is sore and dry. I'm so thirsty.

I push myself up to a sitting position, and I hate every second of moving. But I don't think anything is broken. My aunt holds onto my arm, giving me extra support.

"You can call me Auntie, or Michelle. You don't need to be so formal." She bends down to fluff my pillows, then hugs me gently, if not a little awkwardly.

Her voice is almost familiar. Then I remember why. A month before Mom and I moved, we got a call. I'd answered the phone, and hers was the voice on the line. She called me by name then, but I was too distracted running out the door to wonder about it until later. I wonder why Mom hadn't told me it had been her. I would have liked to talk to her. Then again, I suppose after that call, Mom had been quieter than normal. I didn't want to press her when she seemed to have so much on her mind, so I just never asked. I forgot it soon enough.

"What happened?" I ask. I don't know what hospital this is or how I got here. There's a fog surrounding my mind, making it hard to think.

Michelle frowns, and the fingers of her hand gripping her purse strap tighten until her knuckles lose color. Then she looks up at the doctor as he walks into the room. She doesn't answer my question. I stare at her, waiting for one anyway. But she keeps her gaze locked on the doctor.

My head hurts too much to think clearly.

The doctor—my eyes flick to his name tag: Dr. Underwood—starts talking to my aunt Michelle. After a few seconds, I tune them out, resting my head back against the pillows. I close my eyes, and when I open them again, I'm unsure if several minutes have passed, or just several seconds.

He fusses, and I barely give him a passing glance as he checks my pulse, eyes, throat. He's average height, with salt-and-pepper hair and blue eyes that I'd normally drool over. But not today. Today I just want to keep my head from splitting open from the pain.

Michelle puts her purse in her lap as she sits down on the chair next to my bed, waiting for the doctor to do his thing.

"How do you feel, Miss Price?" he asks.

I hate that my last name is different from Mom's. Always have. I never understood why she gave me my dad's name and not hers, when he hasn't been around since before I was born. Even hyphenating would have been preferable; then at least I could request people use Baker.

I purse my lips and want to give a smart-ass answer, but I hold my tongue. He's only doing his job. Besides, it's only the drumbeat of my pulse pounding at my temples that's making me irritable.

"Not great. My head hurts," I mutter, and because I still want an answer, I add, "What happened?"

"You and your mother were in a car accident, sweetie," Michelle says. The quietness of her voice doesn't suit her.

I jerk up to sit straighter and wince at the pain. "What? Where's Mom? Is she okay?"

My heart thumps, and I can feel each beat hammering in my skull.

Michelle looks to the doctor like she's afraid she's said too much. That look has me worried. *What isn't she telling me? Whatever it is, it can't be good.*

"Can you remember anything about what happened?" the doctor interjects. He must have perfected his bedside manner, because he doesn't look the slightest bit concerned.

I think back. I remember Mom wanting to move to some small town in Colorado I'd never heard of for her job. We were going to stay with an aunt I'd never met before, who is obviously Michelle. I remember packing my things into the car and hoping the movers wouldn't get lost, the vast hours of straight road with next to nothing to look at once we left Oregon, how it was even worse after we crossed through that small corner of Utah, and it was pitch black out with only the blinding headlights from other cars . . . But that's it.

I shake my head, then instantly regret the movement. I hope a nurse comes by with pain meds soon. I don't think I can rest until this pain dies down.

"Don't worry too much about it. You just woke up. Sometimes temporary amnesia of the event can happen. You're very lucky—no broken bones, just some bruising." Dr. Underwood writes on my chart as he talks.

And aching muscles that feel like I've been deadlifting a moose, I think.

"What day is it?" I ask.

"It's the ninth," the doctor says, his pen not even pausing.

It's been two days since we left.

"When can I go home?" I ask. If I have to lay around and be in pain, I'd much rather it be somewhere less sterile looking.

"I would like you to stay the night, but barring any issues, you should be able to go home in the morning."

"What about my mom?" I push. Panic presses down on my chest.

His face is neutral. Not happy, but not the face of having to deliver *really* bad news. "Ms. Baker is stable, but she isn't awake yet, which is for the best. She has quite a few injuries, so we are isolating her for the time being. It will allow her to heal faster without risk of infection. I am confident she'll wake up in the next few days." A strange look passes over his face.

I sit back and breathe. The tightness in my chest eases. Just a bit. She's not in critical condition, so I'm glad for that, though this is far from what I'd hoped to hear.

The doctor puts my chart back at the foot of my bed and says, "I'll be back to check on you later. Visiting hours are only for another few minutes."

Then he leaves the room.

I just want to go home, to sleep in my bed in good old Boring, Oregon. I don't know where we are, but I know this isn't home. "What town are we in?"

Michelle—because even though she's my aunt, I don't know her well enough to think of her like that. Not yet—stands and looks at the clock as she slides the purse strap over a shoulder.

"You're in Havenwood Falls." I must make a face, because she clarifies, "Colorado. The car crashed just outside of Grand Junction, a few hours from here. I had you both brought here when I heard what happened."

I stare dumbly at her. I guess I don't remember *anything* after somewhere in the middle of Wyoming. Did I fall asleep? Mom must have been driving for hours while I was unconscious.

"Get some rest," she says, hugging me again. "I'll be back for you in the morning."

Then she leaves, and I'm alone. I scoot down into the bed, pull a pillow from behind my head, and hug it tightly to my chest.

I don't want to be here, away from my home, my things, and without my mom.

Purchase **Cast in Moonlight** where books are sold.

www.ingramcontent.com/pod-product-compliance
Lightning Source LLC
Chambersburg PA
CBHW051958170626
46808CB00007B/2681